"Of course," Quequex said, "we may never be certain what lies on the far side of the Gate of Worlds.

"The Gate of Worlds?" I asked.

"You do not know what that is?"

I shook my head.

Quequex smiled and looked at the moon, and his face took on the crafty expression of the professional sage. "The Gate of Worlds," he said in a portentous voice, "is the gate beyond which all our futures lie. For each of us at any time many futures lie in wait. And for each possible future, there is a possible world beyond the Gate."

Mystified, I said, "The more you tell me, the less I understand."

Quequex ripped a dozen blades of grass from the ground. He laid down and arranged the others so that each radiated from it at an angle.

"This," he said, pointing to the edgewise blade, "is the Gate of Worlds. And these"—he indicated the blades at angles to it—"are the possible worlds coming forth on the farside of the turning point."

Robert Silverberg
The Gate of Worlds

TOR
A TOM DOHERTY ASSOCIATES BOOK

THE GATE OF WORLDS

Copyright © 1967 by Robert Silverberg

Published by arrangement with the author.

A TOR Book

Published by Tom Doherty Associates, 8–10 West 36 Street, New York, N.Y. 10018

Cover art by Mike Embden

First TOR printing: August 1984

ISBN: 0-812-55454-X
CAN.ED. 0-812-55455-8

Printed in the United States of America

For Robert A. Heinlein

CONTENTS

THE GATE OF WORLDS

ONE

ACROSS THE OCEAN SEA

SOME day soon—maybe by 2000—they'll finish inventing the flight machines, and people will be able to cross the Ocean Sea the way the birds do, in a couple of days. But in that year of Grace 1985 of which I mean to speak, no such fancinesses were yet available. I came to the New World the sober way, by ship.

A long and stormy crossing it was, too, and I hated every moment of it. But before I grumble to you of it, let me tell you something of myself. I have no assurance that this document will have any readers at all, of course. Myself excepted. I write it for myself, to get my recollections down on paper and perhaps to sort out the many things that happened to me while I was in the Hesperides.

But who knows? This may become a prized work of world literature, translated even into Turkish and Arabic. And in that case I had best identify myself at the outset:

Dan Beauchamp, Esq. Late of the city of New Istanbul, which I prefer to think of as London. Born on August 16, 1967, which made me just about eighteen years old at the time that I undertook this voyage. Height: five feet, eleven and three quarters inches, no matter how much I try to stretch. Weight: one hundred seventy-five pounds. Complexion: fair, with blue eyes, blonde hair. No one will ever mistake me for a Turk.

You have noted already that I have a certain aversion to using the Islamic calendar. Nor do I use Moslem weights and measures, despite these things being customary in Europe as a legacy from our Turkish masters. The Beauchamps have a long history of independence. Back in the seventeenth and eighteenth centuries, when any Englishman with common sense was bowing five times a day to Mecca and muttering his Mussulman prayers, the Beauchamps were hiding in London cellars to celebrate the Mass. After the Turks went away, most of the customs they had imposed on their European subjects remained. But you'll not find a Beauchamp asking Mohammed for favors!

If I was that fond of England and English ways, you ask, why was I bound for the Hesperides?

Very simple. A matter of money.

Europe is no place for a likely lad to seek

fortune, or even fame. Europe is a feeble place
indeed, bowed under six centuries of woe. A man
must turn to other shores. To Africa, maybe, or
else to the Hesperides.

I chose the western world. That's what Hesperides
means, I smugly point out here: *western*. Two big
blobs of land in the middle of the Ocean Sea,
sitting between Europe and the Indies. The Upper
Hesperides, the Lower Hesperides, and that skinny
snake of land called the Middle Hesperides. Of
course, the natives have their own names for these
continents. But an Englishman who calls Roma
"Rome" and Firenze "Florence" is not going to
fill his mouth with the Nahuatl or Quechua names
for the western lands, when he has a lovely name
like "the Hesperides" right at hand.

Mind you, I wasn't sailing west for abstract
reasons. My family was bankrupt. My father, who
stands six feet seven and in a better world would
be a king, at the very least, had gone into a
coal-mining venture in the Midlands. The new
factories of our belatedly industrialized land were
hungry for coal, and a man who offered to supply
those greedy boilers was certain to be rich. Except
for my father, who clearly bears the mark of Allah.
Wouldn't you know that he'd tap an underground
river the moment his men began to dig? A flooded
mine, six workers drowned, half a meadow collapsed, and a scandalous worry of lawsuits—that
was my father's coal venture!

So the money was gone. My older brother Tim

signed on for five years in the Janissaries, and today is one of the Sultan's Christian legionnaires, doing battle against the soldiers of the Pasha of Egypt. My sister Sal covered her embarrassment at the bankruptcy by making a swift marriage to a Russian diplomat. That was in 1984; now she's living at the court of the Czar, no doubt shivering most of the time.

That left me. For a few months I stayed at home, but I couldn't stand it. I'd watch my father slam his fists against the wall in anger and frustration, and then I'd wait for the house to cave in, for my father has never been one to smite gently. I couldn't abide the curdled look of sorrow and rage that he wore all the time. Simply dumping some coal in the furnace on a cool day would open all his wounds, and he'd bleed gallons over his bankruptcy.

So I left. I had a few ducats hidden away, and I pulled them forth and bought passage on the *Xochitl*, an Aztec steamer plying the route from Southampton to Mexico. I didn't run away from home, as some might have done. I told my family plainly and clearly what I wanted to do.

"To go to the Hesperides," I said. "To make some money and win some land. I could become a prince among the Aztecs."

"What makes you so sure?" my father asked, now seeing defeat staring through every window. "They're a hard lot. They'll cut out your heart for you, that's what they'll do!"

"Oh, Dad, they quit that game a million years ago!"

"I doubt it. Mexico runs red with blood. Go to Peru, if you must."

I knew that I had won my way, if he was now merely trying to influence my choice of destination. So I laughed and said, "I've studied the wrong language for that, Dad! I don't know the Inca tongue at all, but I've practiced my Nahuatl for months."

"You've been learning the Aztec speak on the sly?" he asked, surprised. "I don't believe it!"

I grinned and reeled off a sentence in Nahuatl, full of the shushing sounds and liquid trills that make that language such an unholy terror. I doubt that Moctezuma XII would have understood what I said, but my father looked awed, and he's not a man to awe easily.

"What did you say?" he asked.

"That I would come home from Mexico a rich man," I told him proudly.

And thus I departed. It was the eve of King Richard's coronation, but I couldn't stay for the fun, for my ship was to leave. I crossed England in a foul, smoky, rumbling monster of a railroad and arrived at Southampton the next day, covered with soot. The station signs still said Port Mustapha. It is nearly sixty years since the Turks were driven from England, and yet you'll find their pagan names sticking to the land everywhere. A mark of a weakened country, that's what it is. Port Mustapha, indeed!

The *Xochitl* was at anchor off her pier. And a magnificent sight she was, too.

The Aztecs have become the world's leading maritime nation, followed by Russia and Japan. I hear the Incas are building a fleet, these days, as a ploy in their war of nerves with their Mexican rivals. But as of now, if you want to cross the Ocean Sea, you do it in an Aztec vessel.

What I saw before me, riding high out of the water, was a superb white-hulled steamer with twin paddlewheels. They were huge wheels, probably bigger than they needed to be, for the Aztecs were ever fond of display. Along the flanks of the ship they had painted the glowing, gaudy images of their revolting deities. There was horrid Huitzilopochtli with his crocodile head, and Xipe Totec, the Flayed God, and Quetzalcoatl, the Feathered Serpent. And near the bow was a hideous depiction of snaky Coatlicue, the mother-goddess. The Aztecs think of her approximately as we Christians think of the Virgin Mary, but I cannot see how they can have tender thoughts of that nightmare figure. However, it is not my business what kind of gods the Mexican lads choose to honor, I suppose.

The *Xochitl's* sails were rigged, which meant the ship was close to departure. A full array of canvas fluttered in the breeze, and, of course, the sails were covered with a further collection of sacred monstrosities. It comforted me only slightly to know that those toothy horrors were going to protect us on our voyage.

I shouldered my knapsack and joined the line of those boarding the ship.

Most of my fellow passengers were wealthy Aztecs going home after a tour of picturesque Europe. They were dressed in complete regalia: feather capes, gold headbands with feathers in them, ear-plugs and nose-plugs, golden anklets and wristlets, and flowing cotton robes. There was a time when Aztecs dressed in simple modern clothing like ordinary folks. But since Mexico became so powerful in world affairs, the Aztecs have revived some of their old customs, not including human sacrifice. And today they parade around as though in masquerade, decked out in the costumes of their bloodthirsty ancestors.

There were some Peruvians getting aboard, too. I was a bit surprised at that, in view of the bad blood currently existing between Mexico and Peru. But there's no actual state of war, just a kind of frozen hostility, and I suppose the Aztecs are glad to take a little Inca money. The Incas were tightlipped and obviously unhappy at having to sail home on a foreign boat, but it's their own fault for having been so slow at setting up their own oceanic navy. They wore austere white robes and no decorations at all, as though trying to show the too-colorful Aztecs up as vain fools.

The rest of the ship's population, about ten

percent of the passenger list, was miscellaneous. A couple of African businessmen who, I would guess, came from the Mali Empire. A wizened little Russian merchant. A pair of Spaniards, chattering away in Arabic. A couple of Turks, perhaps ambassadors to Moctezuma's court. A plump tourist couple from Ghana. And a few miscellaneous natives of the Upper Hesperides, bound home the long way. I was the only Englishman on board. Since everyone else was more or less swarthy, ranging from copper-color to midnight black, I felt more conspicuous than otherwise.

Aztec crewmen saw us on board. I was shown to my cabin, in the steerage, of course, and shared with three other voyagers. My companions were redskins from the Upper Hesperides. They grinned at me in a good-natured way and greeted me in Turkish, which was the only European language they comprehended.

I would sooner have spit out all my teeth than speak a syllable in Turkish. So I answered their greeting in Nahuatl.

They looked surprised; then they looked angry; and finally they looked pleased. My tactic was understood. They had spoken to me in the language of Europe's hated former masters. And I had replied to them in the language of the detested, all-powerful Aztecs who run not only Mexico but much of the rest of the Upper Hesperides. Fair was fair; their pain was my pain.

After that we got along wonderfully well.

One of them produced a bottle: Aztec liquor, the fiery stuff they make from fermented cactus juice. He grinned from ear to ear and shoved the bottle at me.

Now, I am not very fond of alcoholic beverages. I drink them for political reasons. That is to say, the Turks are forbidden by their religion to drink strong waters, and so any Turk-hater worth his hide will gladly take a drink. I will also drink for social reasons, as when a grinning stranger with whom I must share a small cabin for many weeks hands me a bottle. But I do not care for the dizzying effects of the stuff. The world is hard enough to cope with when your mind is clear; I can't see fogging your brain at all.

Except, as noted, for political or social reasons. I took the bottle, put it to my lips, and reared my head back. Then I admitted a small but visible quantity of the liquor to my throat, gasped politely, and handed back the bottle. The three redskins stamped the floor in pleasure. A moment later one of them produced a knife. I wondered if I had given offense, and got ready to sell my life for a dear price.

But he didn't mean to fight. He kicked aside the straw mat on the floor of our cabin and quickly scrawled a passable map of the Upper Hesperides. Then he put a deeply incised X on it, about two inches inland from the peninsula that sticks out of the southeast corner of the continent.

"We live there," he said—in Nahuatl.

I nodded to show I understood.

"You visit us?" he asked.

"I would like to," I said, although I had no special intention of setting foot on their part of the Upper Hesperides at that moment.

He drew a circle around the X, in case I hadn't noticed it. "Here. Our home. Near the sea."

The other two stamped on the floor in delight. The bottle of firewater was passed again.

Then I was handed the knife.

I thought they wanted me to show them where I lived, now. So I sliced a map of the British Isles into the floor and put an X at London.

"Yes," they said. "New Istanbul."

"London," I corrected sharply.

And as men who had lost their own independence, and knew what it was like, they apologized in halting Nahuatl and said, "Yes. London. London."

I handed back the knife. The man who seemed to be the leader shook his head and pressed it into my hand. A gift? No. He gestured as if throwing. What? A game? Yes Yes. A game. A pleasant game of knife-throwing to while away the weary hours.

Well, why not?

Like any sensible boy I had wasted many irreplaceable moments of my life doing pointless things like throwing knives. So I took the redskin blade in my hand and studied it a moment. It was longer than I was accustomed to, and the butt was thick and heavy. Lightly I wrapped my fingers over the cool metal. I brought my hand behind my back and cut loose.

I had misjudged the distance. The knife went end-over-end, hit the beam I had been aiming at butt first, and bounced off with a little clunking sound. My new friends smiled as if they were embarrassed for my sake. I picked up the knife again.

The secret of throwing knives is to get the knife spinning in such a way that it hits the target point first, moving fast. I calculated that I had given it half a spin too much. I tried again.

Thwick! The blade was deep in the wood.

It stayed there. Another knife was pressed into my hand. I threw it.

Thwick! It lodged half an inch away from the first.

I accepted a third blade, cocked my arm, let it fly.

Thwick! Now there was an equilateral triangle of knives embedded in the cabin wall.

My copper-hued comrades cheered wildly. The fire-water bottle was passed once more. The knives were pulled from the wall and I was asked to demonstrate my skill again.

Thwick! Thwick! Thwick!

I had found the range. So far as I was concerned, I could stand there throwing the knife into the wall exactly where I wanted it to go until we reached Mexico.

After a while, the others started taking their

turns. It soon was obvious that they were all expert knife-throwers. They were just as good as I was. But there was no surprise in that. The surprise was for them, to discover that I was their equal with a blade. They were awed by that, I could tell. They had not expected a white man to handle their weapon so expertly. But all those hours of misspent youth had served me in good fashion.

An hour later, the bottle was empty and the cabin wall was covered with little nicks. The voyage, I thought, had started well.

But of course the voyage had not started at all. We were still at harbor in Southampton.

The cabin door opened and a haughty Aztec stuck his head in, without bothering to knock. From the way he was dressed and the way he sneered at us, he could easily have been King Moctezuma's younger brother. But all he was, really, was a lowly ship's steward.

He snapped in Nahuatl, "Your papers?"

We produced our documents. He studied them a moment, brusquely crumpling them as he handed them back. He looked at the three redskins as though they were cattle, and looked at me as though I were some kind of strange animal with a particularly vile odor. His arrogant gaze took in the knives and the sliced-up wall, and his mouth quirked as if he were saying to himself that nothing better could be expected from such beasts, anyhow. Then he said, "We sail in half an hour. You eat when the bells ring."

He went out.

One of my friends flipped his knife at the door as it closed. If the Aztec had still been standing there, he'd have had the blade through his Adam's apple. We laughed.

Take this as a bit of easy wisdom: people who try to rule over other people are going to be hated. That's true of Turks in Europe, of Incas in the Lower Hesperides, of Aztecs elsewhere in the New World, of Russians in Asia. So if you happen to belong to a ruling race, try a little courtesy when you're in the presence of the ruled. You're likely to live longer that way. I could have spitted that Aztec steward myself, and he had done nothing more serious to me than bestowing a fishy stare.

We headed up on deck to watch the departure. The anchor was hoisted; the sails bellied out; the paddlewheels began to turn.

I took a last look at England's green and pleasant land.

Then the *Xochitl* moved in stately fashion out of the harbor and toward the endless Ocean Sea. It tooted its horn in farewell.

I stared at the water that lay ahead. Somewhere far before me the sun was dipping into the sea, and golden streaks shimmered along the waves. Ahead lay a strange world, but at least a different world, where I stood a fair chance of fulfilling my dreams.

Someone nudged my side. It was one of my knife-throwing friends. He nodded in the general direction of a towering Aztec seaman and said, "We push him off?"

"I don't think it's a good idea."

We went below. The ship steamed westward. That night I dreamed I was in the palace of Moctezuma, and the King took me by the hand, and called me Dan, and said he was glad I had come to visit his country.

TWO

THE REALM OF MOCTEZUMA XII

I WILL resist the temptation to describe my ocean crossing in detail.

It was an unpleasant experience, and I see no reason to inflict that experience on any readers I'm lucky enough to have. Besides, describing the voyage would mean reliving it, and I'm not keen to do that.

So let's just say that it was six weeks that seemed like six months, full of gray, tossing seas, surging waves, cold rain, and other discomforts. I was seasick for the first two weeks, which is just as well, since it meant I heaved up the Aztec food before it got very far into my digestive system. After a while I got my sea legs and stopped heaving, and as a result came down with a variety of stomach miseries from that food. Then I got used to the food. But I never got used to the idea of living in a little wooden box tossed around on the surface of the sea.

My chief comfort was that few of my shipmates got used to it either, including the sailors. Aztecs are not seamen by inclination; they go to sea for reasons of national pride, but that doesn't mean they like it. Your Portuguese, your Spaniard, your Italian—those are your sailors. But, like the good Moslems they are, they do their sailing in an easterly direction from Europe. I rejoiced in seeing the long-legged Mexican sailors unloading their dinners at the leeward rail. (I learned very quickly that it's not such a good idea to heave to windward.) But it was a pale pleasure to watch them, seeing as how I felt.

I spent a good deal of my time throwing knives with my bunkmates. Good simple folks that they were, they were willing to toss knives eighteen hours a day, until our cabin wall was thin as paper and the chips were ankle deep. But I needed a more complex challenge. I excused myself tactfully and mingled with the other passengers. Since there was no one else on board who would admit to speaking English, I had to speak Nahuatl, and my knowledge of the Aztec language was polished mightily within a few days.

Most of the Mexican passengers, being rich and aloof, wanted nothing to do with a scruffy English boy of no particular importance. But I struck up

some acquaintance with a Peruvian boy of about
sixteen, who was by way of carrying on a shipboard romance with an Aztec girl—love knows no
politics—and through her I met her older brother,
a sleek Mexican brave a couple of years older than
I. He was just rebellious enough toward his par-
ents so that he was willing to talk.

His name was Nezahualpilli. As Aztec names
go, that's a simple one. (Try walking around with
a barbarious mouthful like Ixtlilxochitl! That was
his father's name.) He had done the grand sightsee-
ing tour through Rome, Greece, Turkey, and on as
far as Egypt, and now he was going home to get
married. His intended bride, as far as I gathered,
was fat, dull-witted, and mustached, but her family owned a cacao plantation the size of Yorkshire.
Papa Ixtlilxochitl had arranged the wedding, and it
would be worth Nezahualpilli's inheritance to
complain. Well, that was *his* problem. My problem was that I was going to a brand new world
with six shillings in my pocket and no idea of what
I was going to do, except that I wanted to do
something exciting and important.

"You have nothing arranged for you in Mexico?"
he asked.

"Nothing."

"But what will you do?"

"I don't know."

"We don't tolerate paupers, you see. They'll
arrest you. They'll put you in the army."

"No," I said. "That's not what I'm coming to Mexico for."

"But you have no place to fill," he pointed out.

I admitted it was true. I admitted that I was doing a scatterbrained thing. Essentially I had run away from home. With permission, true, but without any real plan. I had taken off for the Hesperides in the blind hope that good fortune would come my way.

I said, "Well, if you were in my place, what would *you* do?"

Nezahualpilli considered that for a moment. Then he replied, "The first thing would be to go to Tenochtitlan. The capital is where things happen. Then I would seek out some young, ambitious member of our royal family and attach myself to his service. After that, anything could occur. We have many restless young princes. They frequently plan military adventures. It could be to your profit to join the right one."

"Can you tell me the name of a man to look for in Tenochtitlan?"

He shrugged. "I am not from that city. I do not meddle in such things. I simply offer the suggestion, for what it may be worth."

Nezahualpilli would go no further, and I didn't press him. He was all right, for an Aztec. But, as I learned later on, he wasn't really an Aztec, for he came from Texcoco, a city east of the big lake in the Mexican heartland. Texcoco was a great city long before the Aztecs gave up chewing mud in the highlands, and even now, six centuries later, its people look down on the Aztecs as interlopers. Nezahualpilli invited me to visit him when I reached Texcoco. "I will introduce you to my new wife," he said gloomily.

I pondered his advice as our ship neared Mexico. The more I thought about it, the more I liked it. Yes: go to some bold prince and say, "I'm here to serve you. Arthur of Britain's blood is in my veins. Richard the Lion-Hearted is my ancestor, too. And James the Valiant, who swam the rivers of Turkish blood. Take me into your service and we'll grow great together." Yes. That was the way.

We were in tropic seas now. The sun, a great swollen yellow eye, seemed to take up half the heavens. I began to worry about what that searing radiation was going to do to my fair Anglo-Saxon skin, accustomed as it was to an England in which cloudy days are the rule of life. I decided to expose myself a little at a time, and this, with some suffering along the way, turned the trick. Within ten days I could stand the sunlight except at the midday hours, and my white skin was tanning swiftly.

It had just begun to seem as though the voyage would never end when the word was passed that we were landing at the Mexican port of Chalchiuh-cueyecan. No, I didn't invent that name, nor do I think it's particularly hard to pronounce, now that I've spent some time in Mexico. Take it a syllable at a time and you'll be all right, more or less. It's

in the province of Cuetlaxtla, which is on the east
coast of that narrow part of Mexico just before the
land widens into the Middle Hesperides.

It was hot. I had never known such heat before.
It was as if a blanket lay over the world here.
When I drew the air into my lungs I felt them start
to sizzle. Sweat oiled my skin. Looking through
the sweltering haze toward shore, I saw the greenness
of unknown trees, and a low swampy plain stretch-
ing toward the horizon. They had warned me that
parts of Mexico were hot, but I was unprepared for
such infernal heat. I prayed that the interior of the
country would be cooler. I have never been fond
of heat; if I must confess it, I picked Mexico over
Africa simply on grounds of the climate. And as
we prepared to land at Chalchiuhcueyecan, I was
wondering if I had made a mistake.

The ship approached shore, its paddlewheels
slowly and solemnly revolving. Nezahualpilli came
up to me, fully clad in his Aztec finery now, pearl
ear-plugs, and war paint and feathered cape and
all.

"Have care," he said. "The gods go with you.
Perhaps this will help."

He thrust something into my pocket and strode
away.

I pulled it out. It was a roll of paper money,
Mexican currency, every bill bearing its own gaping-
mouthed divinity. He had given me upwards of a
dozen gold cacaos, the gold cacao being worth
nearly two pounds sterling, or three ducats in the

Turkish reckoning. That is to say, Nezahualpilli had handed me as much as an English workingman hopes to earn in a healthy year.

Charity? Dan Beauchamp take *charity?*

I was going to run after him and stuff his money down his throat. Then I thought better of it. I have always been a reasonable fellow, once I overcome my first hot reactions. To Nezahualpilli, the money represented nothing more than light pocket-cash; his jewelry alone probably cost a hundred times what he had given me. On the other hand, I had only a few shillings jingling in my pocket, and unless I could sell them for their silver value they wouldn't be worth a thing in Mexico. I had come here penniless, vaguely hoping that luck would ride with me. Now that luck had thrust a dozen gold cacaos into my pocket, how could I take offense? I silently thanked Nezahualpilli for his generosity, and went below to collect my belongings.

An hour later, I stepped ashore on Mexican soil.

I expected things to be different and they were. This was, after all, the New World. Europeans have been fascinated by this hemisphere since Diogo Lobo was blown across the Ocean Sea in 1585, en route from Portugal to Africa, and I was no exception. I stood entranced by the unfamiliar trees and flowers, the squat buildings, the hideous idols mounted at the end of the pier, the brown naked children running around, the spicy smells of cooking food. A New World indeed! I was glad I had come, despite everything.

"Customs!" a rough voice bellowed in my ear. "On line for customs!"

Customs is a custom I could well do without. I haven't traveled much, but it's enough to make me hate the nonsense of conferring with the bureaucracy every time one crosses a boundary. In Europe it can be a devilish thing, especially if you're traveling in the Teutonic States, where every mile or two you enter a new sovereign nation and have to go through the process all over again. Here, presumably, I'd only have to pass through the business once, but that was once too many.

The debarking passengers formed a long, long line. Native Mexicans, and there were a lot of them, were at the head of it. Then came passengers from politically sensitive and powerful countries, like Peru, Turkey, Russia, and Ghana. Lastly were the citizens of unimportant countries: the Spaniards, the various Upper Hesperides travelers, and myself. It took a minute or so to clear each passenger through customs, and there were five hundred passengers, all but a dozen of them ahead of me, and three customs officers.

Three hours later, well fried from standing in the sun with no roof over me. . . .

"Passport!" the customs man barked.

He said it in Turkish, which he assumed I knew, since every European speaks that language in addition to his own. He was a huge, slender Aztec dressed in a white tunic and the usual decorations. His bare chest, gleaming with sweat, was the color of old vellum. I glowered at him sullenly and produced my passport.

Unfolding it, he looked at my picture, then at me. "Dan Beauchamp?"

"That's right," I said in his own language.

Obstinately, perhaps deliberately to wound, he went on speaking Turkish. "Nationality?"

"English."

"Length of stay in Mexico?"

"I'm not sure," I answered, still talking Nahuatl. "Perhaps indefinite."

"Are you making fun of me?"

"I don't understand."

"Speak Turkish!"

"I'm not a Turk."

"You're European, aren't you?"

"I'm an Englishman. Shall I speak to you in English?"

"Speak Turkish!"

I said several things to him in English, fine old words that I wouldn't care to repeat here. Then I held my breath. If he understood English, I might find myself spreadeagled on a sacrifice stone with a priest groping inside my chest for my heart. But he didn't understand.

"What was that?" he asked.

"I said in English that since I'm an Englishman, I won't speak Turkish. I understand Nahuatl. I'll speak to you in that tongue."

Like all bureaucrats, he was bewildered by an unpredictable development. Europeans weren't supposed to speak the Mexican language; they were supposed to speak Turkish. Very much off balance and looking as though he'd love to put me on the next boat to Southampton, he said in his own language, "Why have you come to Mexico?"

"Military service."

"We have no need of white-skinned soldiers."

"You haven't seen me fight yet."

He scowled, revealing a set of elegantly stained teeth dyed according to current Aztec theories of beauty. "Entry denied," he said. "You have no tourist visa. You have no work permit. We have no use for you here."

"But—"

"A ship sails for Europe in seven days. Until then you will remain in detention."

He turned around to beckon to a pair of ugly, sinister guards armed with lances and pistols. I had a vision of myself dragged away to some loathsome cell and kept penned up until I could be flung aboard the next homeward liner. It would be a trifle humiliating to show up in London next month with the news that the Aztecs hadn't let me in.

The situation called for a little improvisation.

While he was trying to get the attention of the guards, I picked my passport from his desk and slid one of Nezahualpilli's banknotes in it. Then I said loudly to the customs man, "If any harm comes to me, Prince Axayacatl will hear of this."

The mention of King Moctezuma's son and heir

brought the customs man around to face me again. Suddenly he looked a little wan under all that showy paint.

"Who?"

"Axayacatl," I repeated smugly, hoping I was pronouncing the name at least approximately right. That "x" is a "sh," and the sound is something like Ah-shah-YAH-catl. I added, "The Prince is hiring Englishmen for his private bodyguard. Didn't you know that? He sent all the way to England for me, and he won't like it if you treat me poorly."

I reeled that off so glibly that he looked convinced. But then he hesitated and said, "Can you prove this? Where is a document from the Prince?"

"Here."

I handed him the passport again.

He opened it and discovered that shiny brown banknote. Abruptly his hand came up with what must be an automatic gesture of all public officials, and long spidery fingers closed over the bill. He shut his fist. The hand went out of sight, and the bill went with it.

Then he picked up a wooden stamping block, dipped it in a bowl of ink, and stamped my passport. I was free to enter Mexico.

"Good luck in the service of the Prince Axayacatl," he called after me as I passed through the customs shed.

On the other side I waited a few minutes more while my three knife-wielding redskin companions were checked out. They had no difficulties, and when they emerged we hugged each other goodbye and reminisced a while over our journey together. They made me promise to visit them if I ever came to their part of the world, and I solemnly vowed I would. Then the oldest and most articulate of them—his name was Opothle—pressed his sheathed knife into my hand and insisted that I take it.

"No. I couldn't possibly accept."

"I wish it. You will need it. It is a good knife, a fine knife. It carries good spirits."

"But—"

"It was the knife of my grandfather's grandfather."

"That's exactly why I can't take it."

Opothle's eyes hardened. He pushed my hand away as I tried to give him back the weapon. I began to sense that I was insulting him by refusing the gift.

"You will take the knife," he said. It was an order. If I still balked, I might very well find myself in a fight.

"I will take the knife," I agreed. "I am deeply grateful. I can't tell you how honored I am."

"When you are in our country, you will visit us," Opothle said gravely. He punched my shoulder lightly in a gesture of farewell. Then he walked away.

Shrugging, I strapped the sheath of the knife to my belt and pulled out the blade. It was a superb weapon, of course. I would never forget the satisfying *thwick!* as it sliced into the cabin wall. Under the blazing Mexican sun such a knife might well be useful. I nodded my thanks once more to Opothle's retreating form.

Then I sheathed the knife and started to walk into the town.

New World or not, port cities are all alike. There is the waterfront, with its piers and sheds, its warehouses, its one-faced street lined with brokerage houses and commodity dealers. Then there is the interior, with hotels and business establishments. And far inland are the homes of the people lucky enough to live in lovely Chalchiuhcueyecan.

Half dead from the heat, I made my way through a warehouse block. I needed lodging, first. Then dinner. Then information about the route to Tenochtitlan, high in the cool inland valley of the country.

Youngsters stared at me as if I were a visitor from another world, which in a sense I was. Had they ever seen blonde hair before? Surely there was an English consulate here, this being the main Mexican port of the English-Mexico line. Surely some consular official had golden hair, Nordic hair, the hair that the Angles and Saxons brought to Britain before the dark Norman invaders arrived.

Children ran after me.

"Quetzalcoatl! Quetzalcoatl!" they shrilled.

Of course, The Fathered Serpent, the blonde god out of the east, the white-skinned worker of wonders. The Mexicans have long awaited the return of that vanished god. When the Portuguese discovered Mexico in the reign of Moctezuma III, nearly four hundred years ago, the cry went up instantly that Quetzalcoatl had returned. But the wily old King knew how to deal with gods; he plucked out their hearts on top of the Great Pyramid at Tenochtitlan, and since then the white man has always walked warily in the Hesperides.

"Quetzalcoatl!"

I smiled graciously. In English I said, "I will now blot out the sun in token of my divine nature."

But the sun remained as hot and bright as ever. Perhaps if I had tried it in Nahuatl, it might have worked. But frankly, I didn't have the courage.

The children lost interest in me. I turned a corner and headed for what looked like a public hotel, wondering how I would have paid my way if Nazahualpilli hadn't pressed his money on me.

It was a three-story building, fashioned—as most of them were—of dried mud plastered a bright red with some powdered stone. Just within the door I found a young Mexican maiden as lovely as a cool brook in springtime. She was perhaps three years younger than I, with tawny skin, full lips, bright teeth, and large, round, dark, shining eyes that looked smilingly into my own.

I was unmanned entirely by those eyes. I stood there gaping foolishly for a long moment, cudgelling my brain to find the Mexican words for, "Can I get a night's lodging here?" My mouth opened. My mouth closed. No words came forth.

Then a second Mexican woman appeared, and all was changed.

This one was quite clearly the mother of the first. They had the same eyes, the same features. But the mother was thirty-five instead of fifteen, and that made a world of difference. As I was later to learn, Mexican women age swiftly. Mama had lovely eyes, but she weighed two hundred pounds. I had the sickly feeling that her daughter would take the same route, in the fullness of time.

I found my tongue and asked for a room. Mama seemed a little unwilling to give shelter to a wild man from the east, but I flashed my roll of cash and she melted impressively fast. Daughter took me to a room on the top floor. Nothing luxurious, just four walls and a stuffed mattress, the Mexicans scorning to invent the bed. It was wondrously cool, though, after the furnace heat of the day outside.

"Can I get you anything?" the girl asked. Her voice was husky, and she seemed shy as a forest fawn.

"A bowl of chocolatl right away," I said. "Dinner later."

She brought me the chocolatl: a cold, frothy drink seasoned with peppers and other spices. I drank it down in eager gulps. On my first day out from Southampton I had thought that this dark, foaming stuff was the foulest of the foul, but my tastes had changed. I was coming to like Mexican food, which was just as well, since I stood little chance of tasting Yorkshire pudding and leg of mutton again for a while.

I rested a bit, thinking I'd go out and stroll around the town when the cool of the evening descended. In the meanwhile, I had dinner. The usual Mexican fare: cornmeal bread wrapped around miscellaneous spicy fragments of meat and vegetables. I ate well, and washed it down with more chocolatl. Then I set the soiled dishes outside my room for the girl to take away.

By now night had fallen. I went out for my stroll. Oddly, though, the cool of the evening was an unattainable virtue here. It was not so hot as the day, but it was hotter than I cared for. I returned to my room. A night's rest, I thought, and all would be well.

Stripping, I sprawled out on the mattress—comfortable enough—and warily laid Opothle's knife beside me. You could never tell, I thought. But yet this place seemed calm and peaceful and hospitable. I was weary after my broiling day in the sun on the customs line, and sleep was welcome.

I closed my eyes. I must have slipped into a light doze.

Then a voice cried in tones like thunder, "Help! Murder! Assassins! Quequex is being slain! Help! Help! Help!"

THREE

A Sorcerer, More or Less

It was not my business. It did not have to become my business. This was my first night in a strange land, and alien brawls should not have concerned me. I was safe in my room with the door latched.

On the other hand, a man was howling for help in the hallway. Could I simply lie there and let him be murdered?

On the third hand, it might all be a trap to get me out of my room so that I could be attacked and robbed.

I meditated on all this for what seemed like a long time. Actually it must have been less than a second. Then I realized what I had to do. Scooping up the knife, I ran out into the hall.

Two leggy young bandits were attacking an enormously fat old man who seemed weighed down by tons of jade jewelry. He did not appear to be in mortal peril of losing any of his jade, but he was yelling like a dying whale. One of his attackers was trying to hold him by the arms; the other was trying to pull away the jewelry. The fat one was amazingly spry for his age and bulk, and was lashing out furiously with elbows and heels. Nevertheless, he was in trouble.

"Let go of him!" I barked.

In my excitement I said it in English, but the tone of my voice must have conveyed my meaning. The thief who was yanking at the jade swung around and made an ugly face at me, showing six dozen teeth and a couple of yards of tongue. For the first time I understood that the Aztec idols must have been copied from real life.

He snarled and pulled forth a gleaming blade of obsidian, the volcanic glass. His arm went up as though to throw the knife, and I ducked in underneath it, slapping his wrist hard to spoil his aim, and in the same moment bringing my knife across his bare belly. It wasn't my intention to cut him open, merely to scratch him a little. I succeeded.

He yelped. The old man let out a booming cry of satisfaction. He had been hanging on to the other criminal all this while. Now the other had broke free and came at me. For a moment I faced both of them.

"Look behind you!" I shouted, in Nahuatl this time.

Were they stupid enough to look? Yes. They were stupid enough to look. Both of them turned, and I clunked their heads together hard, at the same time giving the one I had scratched a lusty kick in the small of the back. He went lurching forward and fell on his face, landing hard. The other one was quicker, and swung around again to face me, an obsidian blade in his hand. We crouched and circled each other, looking for an opening. I got the distinct impression that he would kill me if he could, and I made up my mind to put my knife as deep into him as possible.

He feinted with the knife and came up with his left foot, intending to kick me in the face, a deft maneuver practiced by limber-jointed fighters. Unhappily for him, I had anticipated the move, and when that foot came off the floor I seized his heel and gave him a shove. There was the sound of tearing muscles and he went down, dropping his knife. Instantly I followed him to the floor and rested the edge of my blade against his throat.

The first one was stirring, now. I indicated what he would bring upon his companion if he tried any tricks.

"Get up," I told him. "Get out of here, and don't come back."

There was little fight left in him. He rose, rubbing his blood-smeared belly where I had made the light slit in it, and unsteadily walked to the exit ladder that served in place of stairs. I watched until he was gone. Then I heaved my prisoner to his feet and marched him toward the ladder, pressing the knife none too gently into the lump of his throat.

"Down," I commanded. "Go. Fast."

He went. Down. Fast.

Order was restored. Now, and only now, did our bulky landlady arrive to see what had been going on. When she found that the hoodlums were gone, she threw her arms around me and embraced me vigorously. The old man did the same, so that for a dizzying moment I was squeezed between at least five hundred pounds of Mexican flesh.

Then they released me. The landlady announced that my lodging would cost me nothing. She said that bowls of chocolatl would instantly be sent to my room, and stronger drink if desired. The old man, for his part, plucked off a massive pendant of ocean-dark jade and draped it around my neck. I was growing used to receiving gifts by now.

"My savior! My deliverance!" he boomed. "We are companions for life! I owe all to you! Your name?"

"Dan Beauchamp. Of London."

"Quequex is my name," he replied. "I am from the city of Azcapotzalco, but I make my home now in Tenochtitlan. I am a sorcerer to the royal court."

"A sorcerer?"

"A sorcerer, more or less," he said modestly. "As I grow older and fatter, the devils no longer dance to my commands. But Moctezuma doesn't know that yet." He laughed, and the flesh rippled all over him. He was shorter than I by six inches or more, but at least twice as heavy, a small mountain of fat half concealed by baubles of jade. Unlike any other Mexican I had seen, Quequex wore a beard—a stringy one, true—and his round-featured face lacked the sharp cheekbones and jutting nose of the true Aztec. Perhaps he came from some other tribal line.

Wise old eyes stared out from that pudgy face. With the danger gone, he seemed relaxed and mellow, though he had been screeching piteously only ten minutes before. We repaired to his room, and over bowls of chocolatl we struck up an acquaintanceship.

"Where are you bound?" he asked. "What takes you from London?"

I told him my tale. He nodded sagely. "Very good, very good," he wheezed. "A boy should seek his soul in strange worlds. So is it written. You go on to Tenochtitlan?"

"Yes."

"A blessing upon us. We will travel together, Dan Beauchamp. You will protect me from the mountain bandits. And I will instill in you some of the wisdom that great age and extreme corpulence have bestowed on me. Is it agreed? I leave tomorrow."

I hadn't planned to head to the capital so soon. But it seemed to me better to travel in the company of this fat old fraud than to go alone through an unknown land.

We sat together far into the night. He claimed to be on his way back from Peru, where he had gone as a special envoy from King Moctezuma XII to His Imperial Majesty, the Inca Capac Yupanqui V. Although from my brief acquaintance with Quequex I could not imagine why a king would wish to trust him with matters of high diplomacy, I didn't challenge his assertion. Certainly he had been to Peru, for he showed me fine blankets of the Inca weave, and some small silver statuettes that had clearly been made in Cuzco. But I suspected he had gone there for private reasons, not as envoy from king to king.

He questioned me at length about European politics, which seemed to interest him intensely. He knew the political structure of Europe far better than I had expected him to, and spoke with knowledge of the persecution of Christians in Spain and Italy, the proposed merger of a few dozen of the Teutonic States into a United Germany, and the recent friction between the Czar of Russia and the Sultan of Turkey.

"And you?" he said. "A Moslem, are you?"

"Christian, sir."

"Indeed so? How did that happen?"

"My family remained Christian after the Turks conquered England. It's the way we are."

He smiled, creasing his drooping jowls. "Chambers underground where prayers are said. The crucifix in its hidden place. An outward acceptance of Islam. The secret rites: Christmas, Easter, Twelfth Night. Yes?''

"Yes." I felt a stab of nostalgia. Christmas would be coming soon, and all England under a blanket of white snow. While here I was in this torrid land of endless heat, away from home for the first time at the season of the holly and the ivy. "How is it you know so much of our religion? You can't have met many Christians."

"It is my trade to know the holy mysteries of the world," he replied dreamily, rocking gently back and forth, his belly bulging like a Buddha's. "I have been in Jerusalem, do you know? I have seen the birthplace of Christ, and the place where He died. And I have been to Mecca, shuffling round the black rock with the Faithful. In Istanbul once, the Sultan and I—"

Was he a shameless liar? Or had he really done such things? He spoke so glibly.

I could not check him on his tales of carousing in the Sultan's halls. But I could verify him in other ways.

"Have you been to London, Quequex?"

"New Istanbul, so it is usually called. Yes. I was there thirty years ago, for the coronation of King Edward of blessed memory. A cold time it was, too, all snow and pain. I was part of the royal delegation from Mexico." And he proceeded to launch into a lengthy recollection of London. He described it faultlessly: Oxford Street and Piccadilly, the monument to the defeat of the Turks, the Tower, the British Museum, the Grand Palace of Sultan Mahmud, St. Paul's, the Mosque of Ali. Of course, he could have been faking it. But he was convincing. When he told of looking down the Strand and seeing the winter sunlight glinting off the gilded dome of the Mosque of Ali, I felt like weeping, for even a Christian Englishman bears affection for that grand house of Allah that the Turks built in the heart of our city. It is a wonder of the age, and even I who abominate all things Islamic would not tear it down.

We talked far into the night. That is, Quequex talked and I listened, for once I had told my little tale I had nothing left to say. Chocolatl seemed to oil the wheels of his mind, and he reminisced on and on, his voice now a high wheeze, now a deep boom. He told of kings and emperors, of radiant princesses now long dead, of wars and assassinations, of secret and hideous rites carried out even today within the dark Aztec pyramids. I drank it all in. No matter if he was inventing everything as he went; he was a miraculously fine storyteller, and I could hope only that when and if I reached his age, I could spin a yarn as well.

My head throbbed with lack of sleep after a while. I said, breaking into an improbable account of personal services he had rendered Pasha Malik Ismail when in Cairo, "I must rest now. In the morning—"

"Bring your mat here to sleep," he said. "The assassins may return."

I assured him I'd come to his aid if there were any trouble, but he insisted that I share his room. There was no help for it, so I hauled my mat in. He blew out the lamp. I felt sleep engulf me.

Then came the voice of Quequex: "Dan Beauchamp?"

"Mmm?"

"Perhaps it is not my business, but you said no prayer before you closed your eyes."

I had not said bedtime prayers since the age of eight. But Quequex seemed to be expecting them, so I told him, "I uttered a silent prayer."

"A silent prayer will not be heard, will it? Pray for our safety tonight, Christian. Ask your god to guard us both."

Until I did, I knew, I would get no sleep. So I took to my knees, clasped my hands, and wearily implored Jesus, Mother Mary, and Saint Christopher to watch over us this night. Quequex seemed satisfied. I heard him droning an unintelligible invocation to Huitzilopochtli, and after it a shorter prayer in a Mexican language I did not understand. The evils of the night had been properly prayed away. Once more I lay down on my mat.

Sleep descended like a summer storm—all at once.

When I woke, several years later, bright sunlight was pouring through the window and Quequex, enveloped in jade and freshly painted in horrifying designs, stood above me, evidently about to nudge me awake with his toe.

"At last. The sleeper awakens."

I had had terrible dreams of live Aztec gods pursuing me through the streets of Tenochtitlan, teeth gnashing and claws red with blood. But I concealed that and rose to my feet readily enough.

"Have you eaten yet?" I asked.

He laughed. "Yes, I have eaten. And settled my accounts here. And hired a motorcar to take us to Tenochtitlan. Can you drive?"

"I've never driven before."

"It is not hard. I will show you. Eat, now, and then we leave."

The landlady's lovely daughter brought me a hearty breakfast. My soul soared at the sight of her; I wanted to tell her that she was the most beautiful creature I had ever seen, that I loved her, that I wanted her to share my travels and my life. It is a bad habit of mine, falling in love at a glance, but so far I have escaped the worst consequences of it. In any event, I did not tell the girl any of the things I had on my mind, and quite likely it was better that way. In truth she was an elegant thing, delicate and shy and graceful, but behind that flawless exterior she probably had the empty mind of a small-town serving girl, and when I lost interest in staring into those large dark shining eyes I might find her a dreary companion.

As we left the inn, a curious pang of emotion speared me at the thought that I would never see the girl again. In my romantic way I tried to deny the thought, telling myself that fate would bring us together some day, that I would meet her once more further on in my wanderings. I had read stories in which just such a thing had happened.

But life lacks the neatness of a story. I never did meet her again, and now that I have left Mexico it is not likely that I shall. And, of course, it would be awkward now if I did, considering that—

No. I have tried to maintain strict chronological order in this narrative, and so there is to be no jumping forward to talk of that other dark-haired wench whose sparkling eyes ensnared me by the shores of the blue Western Sea. Let her wait her proper turn.

Quequex had indeed rented a motorcar for our trip inland. Coming as I do from an impoverished and unimportant island, I had never ridden in one of these vehicles, though I had once seen the Earl of Warwick drive proudly through Hyde Park in one. They were invented about thirty years ago by some clever German, I believe. The wealthy kingdoms of the Hesperides imported some German engineers to supervise the building of them here for neither the Aztecs nor the Incas have ever had much in the way of skill with machinery. Now they are so common in the New World that they are available for hire at low cost.

"Dare we ride in that?" I asked him.

"Perfectly safe. Perfectly. Come, lad: I'll show

you how to operate it, for the trip is long and old
Quequex can hardly do all the driving.''

I approached the motorcar. I can best describe it
as a small railway locomotive, consisting of a
steam engine mounted on three wheels, two big
ones in back and a smaller one in front. The large
wheels provided the drive; the small front wheel
did the steering, and there was a lever mounted on
it by which it could be turned from side to side. A
seat in front looked just wide enough for Quequex
and myself. In back was a platform on which one
could stand while loading coal into the boiler.

Quequex lit the boiler fire.

''Is that enough coal to get us to Tenochtitlan?''
I asked.

He laughed. ''It's a day's supply. We purchase
more along the way. There are coal depots for the
benefit of travelers like ourselves everywhere.''

The boiler grew hot rapidly. Soon steam was
coming up, and the engine made great booming
sounds as it started. The car was braked, but I
could see it straining eagerly, and half expected it
to spurt away from us at once.

''Let us board it,'' Quequex said.

We loaded our baggage onto the side compart-
ments provided for it, and got into the front seat.
Quequex sat on the driver's side, gripping the
steering lever. Behind us, the boiler rumbled and
burbled ominously, and gave off so much heat that
I could feel my bones softening.

''Attend to me,'' the garrulous sorcerer declared.

"The controls are few and simple. We release the brake,"—he unsnapped a hook near my knee—"and depress the starter pedal, which engages the gears of the engine. You notice that the car instantly goes forward."

I noticed it, all right. As Quequex stepped on the starter, the car started with a ferocious lurch that all but hurled me from my seat. I clung on for dear life. We were rolling down the highway at a speed of perhaps twelve miles an hour. Thick black smoke poured from our smokestack, and occasionally the boiler gave off a roaring trumpeting sound. From the engine came steady explosions.

Quequex tried to look calm, but I could see that he was inwardly troubled by the car's performance. Children were running alongside us, laughing and cheering, but now the car had picked up such speed that it had left our followers behind. It tended to wobble all over the road, too, and Quequex' pudgy hand gripped the steering lever in earnest.

"These new cars," he muttered. "This is the 1960 model—designed for our wild young men. Give me a good, reliable '45 car any time."

"How long does it take to get to Tenochtitlan this way?" I asked.

Quequex' reply was drowned out by an immense barrage of noise from the boiler. In the fierce heat of the day, sitting with my back against that blazing furnace was no pleasure, even with an insulating plate between. I was covered with sweat and soot. I saw Quequex fumbling with the brake, and to my immense relief the car slowed to a halt.

When it had stopped Quequex said, "Now we change seats. I will teach you how to drive."

I would sooner have learned how to ride to Tenochtitlan on the back of a crocodile. But I had no option; it was hardly fair to force Quequex to do all the driving. Trembling only slightly, I took my place in the driver's seat.

"To go left," he said, "you turn the lever to the left. To go right, you turn the lever to the right. To go straight ahead, you hold the lever in the middle. Understand? Good. When you see an obstacle in the road, you apply the brake. Otherwise you drive forward."

The car was quivering like a snaffled horse trying to bolt.

"Release the brake," Quequex said.

I released the brake.

"Depress the starter."

I depressed the starter.

And just like that I was driving.

I hung on to the steering lever and chewed my lower lip a bit as we plunged forward. Luckily the road was straight and wide, for the Aztecs know a trifle about road building, and I'm told their roads are the best in the world, save only for the masterpieces done by the Inca engineers. This was flat countryside, too, with swamps and stinks on all sides, and that vast sun hanging about sixteen feet above us.

The road was wide, but unfortunately not empty. Peasants on donkeys joggled along next to us, occupying the shoulder of the road and paying absolutely no attention to traffic. Occasionally some nobleman on a high-spirited horse would prance by. Horses, like motorcars, are imports from Europe; the Hesperideans had none of their own until we began selling them to them in the seventeenth century. To this day, our Russian friends do a lively business peddling Siberian ponies in the New World. But just now, with mules and donkeys and drayhorses and Arabian chargers wandering all over the road while I was so desperately trying to control the car, I found myself profoundly wishing that we had never entered the horse trade.

When I got in trouble, though, horses had nothing to do with it.

I had been driving perhaps ten minutes, threading my way through the obstacles on the road and magically failing to hit anything. Just ahead of me now was a cart drawn by two plodding llamas, those sawed-off camels from Peru. One llama chose the moment of my approach to stop dead in his tracks.

Unless I changed course rapidly, I'd smash right into the cart at top speed. There was nothing to do but swing over into the eastbound lane, and I did it, pulling the car to the left just in time to avoid the llama-cart.

However, there was no time to see if anything else was occupying the eastbound lane. And of course just as I entered it there appeared another car, the first I had encountered since we had left Chalchiuhcueyecan. It was a low, shiny, sporty model, newer than ours, containing half a dozen lively young Aztec bucks. They had thoughtfully decorated its front end with one of those nightmarish Mexican gods, so that I had a view of red teeth and yellow eyes zooming toward me.

At the last moment they swerved as far as they could to the outside of the road, and I pulled back to my own lane as well as possible considering the presence of the llama-cart. We passed each other with some six inches to spare. The Aztecs shouted multi-syllabled curses at me as they rocketed past.

I began to realize I was still alive. I pulled the car around the llamas, drifted to the edge of the highway, and braked it to a halt. I looked at Quequex. His face was beaded with blobs of bright sweat, and his swarthy skin was nearly as white as mine from fright. But he was in better shape than I was, right then.

When my teeth stopped chattering, I indicated the steering lever to him and walked around to the passenger side of the car.

"It's your turn to drive," I said.

FOUR

The Gate of Worlds

I was glad that Quequex was driving when the boiler exploded.

It happened on the second day of our western journey to Tenochtitlan. We had covered perhaps sixty miles that first day, driving across a flat muddy plain shimmering with heat, passing from a zone of swampy jungle to a zone of barren desert. Despite occasional terrifying moments when the boiler throbbed and palpitated like a diseased elephant, we had no mechanical difficulties with the car.

That night we halted at a small country hostel where I saw Quequex practice some of his sorcery. The room we were given was infested with crawling insects, and until you have seen Mexican insects you simply have not seen insects. These were upwards of an inch long, with legs meaty enough to have visible thighs. From his luggage Quequex produced a small green candle which he lit to the accompaniment of murmured spells. Whether it was the spells or the smells, I don't know, but the insects vanished soon after the fumes of the candle penetrated our room, and we slept soundly.

No witchcraft could save the car the following day, though.

We gave it a fresh load of coal in the morning and set out on the broad highway soon after breakfast. From the start that day the boiler was behaving strangely, delivering itself of odd burbles and wheezes. The engine went by fits and gasps, too, and each time it caught its breath the whole frame of the car shook violently.

Quequex drove the first stint. After an hour he turned the car over to me.

I drove for an hour.

He drove for an hour and a half.

We stopped in sandy, hilly country and had lunch. The usual food, plenty of spice ground into it, and something mildly intoxicating to drink.

I drove for an hour and a quarter after lunch.

He drove for an hour.

We got out and rested under a shady tree for a while, because the engine seemed to be overheating.

I drove a while. He drove a while. Twilight began to fall. The engine began to fail.

It emitted a series of rasping coughs. I looked

back and saw bluish smoke coming from the boiler vent. I told Quequex about it, and he looked, and said something unintelligible under his breath. We drove on, another mile or so, and abruptly the engine whined and the boiler boomed and Quequex slammed on the brake.

"Run for it!" he yelled.

He grabbed his luggage and I grabbed mine and we sprinted for safety. As I've indicated, Quequex was on the ponderous side, and the ground shook beneath his feet, but he ran as he probably had never run before. At one point he was actually moving faster than I was.

From behind us came the sound of a mighty explosion. An instant later I felt hot raindrops striking my skin; the water in the boiler was spraying down on us. We kept on running. At last Quequex flung himself face down on the ground, moaning and groaning, and buried his head in his arms.

But there was nothing more to fear. The blast was over. I looked back and saw the heap of twisted metal that our car had become. It was sad; I had come to like the noisy, smoky beast since learning to drive.

"It happens," Quequex said. "The horseless chariot is still in an early stage of development."

"What do we do now? There aren't any settlements in sight."

"We walk. We purchase horses when horses are seen for sale. We proceed to Tenochtitlan."

"And the car?"

"We leave it where it is. I am an official of the court of Moctezuma; we will settle things without difficulty. A slight payment, perhaps—"

He heaved himself to his feet, and we walked. For a plump old man, he had plenty of rubber in his legs, because we marched at least five miles through gathering darkness before we came to a town, and he complained not a whit. Beneath the blubber and the braggadocio, Quequex was tough.

We bought horses that night. I didn't see any money change hands, but the awed peasants delivered over a swaybacked mare for Quequex and a husky little colt for me, and off we went. We rode till midnight. I was unaccustomed to the Aztec saddle, which is so skimpy that it might as well not be there at all, but my ebony colt was swift and agile, and I enjoyed riding him. Whether he enjoyed being ridden is another matter entirely, into which I made no inquiry. I doubt very much that the red mare enjoyed carrying the corpulent Quequex, but the mare did not complain in any language we understood, and we sped along quite satisfactorily.

When no hostel appeared, Quequex suggested we camp in an open field for the night. There should have been a hostel somewhere on our route, for the Aztecs have borrowed from the Incas the useful idea of spotting accommodations on every royal highway, but we must have missed the last one somehow. Sprawled we out in thick tall cool grass. From the depths of his pack Quequex produced a few cornmeal cakes that he had stowed away at dinnertime, and we munched.

"Huitzilopochtli!" Quequex expostulated, slapping his fat haunches. "Never since my ancestors left the Seven Caves has a man been as tired as I am now!"

We were both tired, but not sleepy. The moon was huge and bright, a coppery plaque nailed to the sky, and the air was too warm for sleeping. We talked, instead, sitting crosslegged in the grass.

Quequex spoke of wonderful Tenochtitlan and of the Aztec nobles who thronged it. I detected in his voice a note of irony when referring to the royal ones; tall they were and handsome, but to Quequex sleek limbs were nothing without a shrewd brain, and I gathered that the nobility was not distinguished for intelligence. Of King Moctezuma XII, though, Quequex had nothing but praise. The King, he said, was a shrewd, dynamic, ambitious monarch who would make Mexico the greatest nation on the planet.

"Of course," he added, "we may never be certain what lies on the far side of the Gate of Worlds. Who knows in truth what the future holds?"

"The Gate of Worlds?" I asked.

"You do not know what that is?"

I shook my head.

Quequex smiled and looked at the moon, and his face took on the crafty expression of the professional sage. "The Gate of Worlds," he said in a portentous voice, "is the gate beyond which all our futures lie. For each of us at any time many futures lie in wait. And for each possible future, there is a possible world beyond the Gate.''

Mystified, I said, "The more you tell me, the less I understand.''

Quequex ripped a dozen blades of grass from the ground. He laid one down and arranged the others so that each radiated from it at an angle.

"This,'' he said, pointing to the edgewise blade, "is the Gate of Worlds. And these''—he indicated the blades at angles to it—"are the possible worlds coming forth on the far side of the turning point.''

"But—''

"Silence and listen! Every time a man makes a decision, he creates new worlds beyond the Gate, one in which he did this, one in which he did that. The peasant ploughs his fields, and halts to slap at a bothersome fly. In one world, he slaps. In another, he does not, but proceeds down the furrow. It makes small difference in that case. But what if the peasant, by halting to swat the fly, avoids the claws of a jaguar lying in wait at the end of the field? In one world, the peasant swats a fly. In another, he goes to the end of the field and perishes. Again, it makes small difference, except to the family of the peasant. The world is unchanged whether he lives or dies. Unless, of course, one of his descendants is to go to Tenochtitlan and murder the king. If the peasant dies, that distant descendant never is born, the king lives out his years, and all is different from the way it would have been if the peasant, pausing to swat, had lived to engender the ancestors of the assassin.''

My head swam with all this talk of probable worlds. Peasants? Jaguars? Assassins?

Ignoring my evident confusion, Quequex swept serenely on with a torrent of further examples.

''The more important the individual, the more complex the working of the Gate of Worlds must be. Consider King Moctezuma. If he lives, he will bring Mexico new greatness. If he slips in his bath tonight and dies, Axayacatl is king, and the future is different. For each of us at every instant the Gate lies open and an infinity of worlds spreads from it.''

''You mean—there is a world in which the car blew up and killed us, and there's a world in which the car didn't blow up at all, and there's a world in which the car didn't work in the first place?''

''Exactly.'' Quequex beamed. ''Also there is a world in which the bandits killed both of us back in Chalchiuhcueyecan. A world in which you were lost at sea before you ever reached Mexico. A world in which you never were born, for your grandfather died in his cradle. A world in which I never was born. A world in which I was King of Mexico. A world in which Mexico was conquered by Europe five hundred years ago. A world in which there were never any men at all, but only green snakes with many legs. A world in which—''

''Stop!'' I cried, dizzied. ''Please stop!''

Quequex laughed. "It shakes the mind, does it not, to peer through the Gate of Worlds?"

It certainly does. For a moment I had looked upon infinity, and that had been no pleasure.

I said slowly, "But some of the possible worlds you spoke of were ridiculous ones."

"Ridiculous, of course. But possible. If man's mind can imagine it, then it exists in the realm beyond the Gate. All possible worlds exist there. An infinity of worlds, created at every moment. Some are all but identical to others. There are a billion worlds in which I have made different gestures with my little finger in the past ten minutes, all other things being the same. There are a billion worlds in which I have arranged my words in slightly different ways while explaining to you, all other things being the same. There are a billion worlds in which—"

I was afraid I had launched him on another trip to infinity, and my head was still rocking from the last one. So quickly I cut him off by asking, "How could some of those far-fetched worlds come into being, though? The one in which Europe conquered Mexico, for example?"

"You don't see how that could happen?"

"Europe? We couldn't conquer anybody. It was all we could do to get rid of the Turks, and even that took hundreds of years and had to wait until the Turks themselves got soft at the core from easy living. So how could we possibly conquer Mexico, of all countries?"

"It could have happened five hundred years ago."

"Impossible, Quequex! Five hundred years ago we were in worse shape than we're in now. The Turks had conquered us, and—"

"That's in *this* world," he said. "But this is not the only world to have come through the Gate. Envision a different kind of world in which you were strong and we were weak."

"I can't see it at all. Unless you throw in a lot of implausible nonsense."

He shook his head. "Think, my young friend. Step by step by step, find the turning points, see the reasons why the worlds split apart beyond the Gate. How well do you know European history?"

"Well enough. I've been to school."

"What does the year 1348 mean to you?"

"The Black Death, of course," I replied instantly.

"Excellent. The Black Death! The plague that entered Europe and destroyed whole cities. Millions of people dead. Between Poland and Britain, six people dead out of every eight. Europe a vast cemetery. Empty roads, empty houses, corpses rotting in the streets, silence everywhere. A great silence. The deathblow of Europe. Two people left alive out of every eight."

"I see!" I burst in. "If the Black Death had hit the Hesperides instead of Europe—"

"Slowly, slowly, slowly. No need to make such a huge shift in events. Let us say that the plague did strike Europe, but not nearly so savagely. One fourth of the population dead, instead of three-fourths. Europe is wounded, but not robbed of all strength. France, England, Spain still have vitality. It takes time to recover, a hundred years until the population is what it was before the plague. But Western Europe does recover. By 1450 it is strong again."

"And when the Turks invade us—"

"You are seeing the pattern now," said Quequex. "In our world the Turks, like the Russians and the peoples of Africa, did not suffer anything like the devastation experienced in Western Europe. So when the Turks moved westward, they met no opposition. By 1420 they take Constantinople, which you know as Istanbul. By 1440 they are in Vienna; by 1460, Paris; by 1490, London. And at the same time the Arabs come out of North Africa and occupy Spain once more, as well as Italy. Then the Turks and Arabs quarrel, and when the smoke clears the Turks are masters of all of Europe except for Russia. And the Russians have done the same thing in the opposite direction, coming down out of Siberia to seize China and Japan and the rest of Asia."

"That's in the real world. But in this other world where the Black Death wasn't as devastating—?"

"Aha! The Turks invade Europe in this other world, but they are thrown back. They are stopped before they pass Vienna. France, England, and Spain are free to reach outward. Portugal too, perhaps. Ships begin to explore the Ocean Sea. Someone goes around Africa and finds India; someone else sails west and discovers the Hesperides.''

"As Diogo Lobo did in 1585.''

"Yes,'' said Quequex. "But the discovery comes earlier. A century earlier, possibly. By 1500, Europeans have reached the New World.''

I tried to capture this vision of distorted history, in which Europe had had strength enough to defeat the Turks and send ships to sea. I knew what the Europe of 1500 had really been like: a dismal, desolate, sickly land, forcibly converted to Islam and suffering under Turkish misrule. The population of London in 1500 had been something like 6,000. How could such a miserable nation send ships overseas?

Quequex went on, "When a few Portuguese sailors came to Mexico in 1585, they were seized and put to death by Moctezuma III. He was a strong, forceful man who knew that strangers were dangers. But what if the Europeans had come seventy years earlier? Moctezuma II was on the throne then. Do you know what kind of man he was?''

"I'm afraid not. Medieval Aztec history—''

"Of course. How would you know? But he was a poet, a dreamer, a mystic. He feared the coming of Quetzalcoatl, the white-skinned god from the east. If Europeans had come to him, would he have flayed them alive? He would not. He would

have bowed down to them and called them gods!
He would have given them Mexico!''

"Perhaps," I said.

"Another thing. Our empire was new at that
time. We had imposed our rule on the states around
us. We had recently conquered Chalco, Coyoacan,
Xochimilco, and dozens of other states, but they
hated us as all conquerors are hated. We had not
even yet subjugated Tlaxcala. If invaders had come,
the vassal states would have risen up in rebellion
against us. They would have allied themselves
with the Europeans and destroyed us. And in Peru
it would have been the same. The Incas, too, were
new masters. Their empire would have collapsed if
Europeans had attacked it in 1515. But by the end
of the century it was too late. The Aztecs and
Incas had consolidated their power. No Europeans
could possibly overthrow them now.''

"What would the world be like," I wondered,
"if England or Spain or Portugal had conquered
the Hesperides in 1515?''

Quequex smiled. "White men would rule the
New World. We would be slaves. Our temples and
pyramids would be gone, and the cross of Christ
would rise everywhere. Perhaps there would be
more machines in the world, for we have never
been so interested in making machinery as you
Europeans. Perhaps there would be flying machines,
and machines that would permit men to talk across
great distances. Who knows?''

"But it did not happen.''

"It did not happen, no. The Black Death shattered Europe. We were granted the extra hundred years we needed to make our power permanent. Today we are the masters here, and the Incas in the south, and so it will remain. You know, you white people might have conquered Africa too. You have the seed of conquest within you. But Africa also was spared your fury and its black kingdoms remain. Perhaps your plague was the vengeance of the gods upon you, to teach you not to invade other lands."

"But we are peaceful people," I protested. "Meek—kind—loving—turning the other cheek—"

"Tragedy made you meek. But what were you like before the plague? Do you know the story of your Crusades? How your soldiers marched into Syria and Palestine as bloody conquerors? *That* was what you were like."

"The Crusades had a religious purpose!"

"Did they? Oh, yes, you Christians wanted Christ's homeland for yourselves. It belonged to others, but you stole it. And in the same way you would have stolen Africa and our lands, all in the name of holiness, if the gods had not broken you. You would have come to us and forced your cross down our throats and killed our kings and burned our temples. But you were prevented from doing it! The gods sent you the plague, and then they sent you the Turks! Instead of being masters, you were mastered! And only now, when it is too late, are you beginning to recover. It is 1985, not 1500. Too late for conquest!''

Quequex' voice had taken on a shrill, unpleasant pitch, and I sensed that this had become something more than a philosophical discussion. It was almost as if he had looked through the Gate of Worlds and had actually seen that other Earth, in which his people were slaves to mine. And real hatred was ripping and inflaming him now.

But of course it had never taken place, that conquest which he denounced so bitterly now. Christian Europe had gone under in the fifteenth century. Aztec Mexico and Inca Peru ruled the Hesperides. In Africa, black men wore the crowns. Why get so excited, then, over a fantasy, a dream, an airy speculation?

He realized after a while that he had lost control, and subsided, becoming once more his familiar ironic, sarcastic, lighthearted, slightly disreputable self. He ceased to assail the imaginary conquest, or to belabor a Europe that could never have remotely begun to do such a thing.

"It is an interesting idea, this Gate of Worlds," I said. "But one mustn't take it seriously. It leads to headaches and disagreeable emotions."

"You are right, Dan Beauchamp. Let us forget all I have said. It is time for sleep, anyway."

We curled up in the grass and closed our eyes. But for me sleep was a long time in coming. I could not free my mind from that vision of a world transformed. My mind seized on it, embroidered on it, until I seemed almost to be looking through the Gate of Worlds myself. I saw both the Hesperides thronged with the descendants of Europeans. Great cities, mightier than London and Paris and Istanbul, mightier even than Tenochtitlan of the Aztecs and Cuzco of the Incas. Flying machines! Motorcars that ran smoothly without exploding! Buildings towering to the sky! And the men with copper-colored skins, the defeated ones, the natives of the Hesperides—driven back into primitive ways, forced to the borders of their world.

Mind you, I had no wish to see the Hesperides conquered by Europeans. As an Englishman who bears the hereditary sorrow of a land throttled by pagan Turks for so many centuries, I could hardly be eager to see other folk under Europe's yoke—except, perhaps, for the Turks. But I had not opened this box of miracles. Quequex had, and I could not help but remain within the fantasy he had built for me. All night long, now dozing, now dreaming, now lying awake with throbbing eyes, I saw that other world.

Once I looked over at Quequex. He lay on his back, hands clasped across his middle, belly slowly rising and falling, faint snores ebbing from his nostrils. No visions tormented him tonight!

Toward dawn my imagination gave me surcease. The cities I had invented—New York, New London, New Paris, New Rome—faded into misty shadows. The next thing I knew it was dawn, and yellow sunlight was splashing into my eyes, and Quequex

was prodding me awake. "It's many miles to
Tenochtitlan, boy. Up! Up and onward!"

"Quequex—?"

"Yes, lad?"

"In all your sorcery, do you know a way to pass
along the Gate of Worlds, to go from world to
world?"

He laughed at me. "I spoke philosophy last
night. The Gate of Worlds is an abstract concept, a
way to understand the myriad turning points of
history. It's not a tangibility. There's no crossing
it."

"Then New York and New London are only
dreams?"

"What are they?"

"Cities I imagined in the New World you spoke
of, where Europeans had conquered."

Quequex tugged at his chins. He said, "Yes,
only dreams. There's no New York. There never
will be. And even if there were, you'd never reach
it. Untether the horses, now, and we'll be on our
way. Breakfast lies miles ahead of us."

FIVE

Tenochtitlan the Proud

The road became steeper, now. We were climbing toward Mexico's hilly heartland. I, for one, was glad to see the sweltering lowlands behind us. The air was cool and clean here, sometimes even a little too cool for comfort, but much to be preferred to the stinking soup that passes for air by the coast.

We now were in the province of Cuauhtochco and plodding northwest across Mexico's middle toward glittering Tenochtitlan. As he neared his home, Quequex became less talkative; he regaled me with little philosophy here. Perhaps the journey had wearied him, or possibly he was uneasy about the reception he'd receive at the royal court.

At night, when we stopped at hostels along the

way, he'd talk a bit of Aztec mythology. A few bowls of chocolatl would get his tongue working, and he'd fill me with stories of the primordial Seven Caves from which all the Aztecs and other Mexicans had originally come, and the paradise they'd left behind to go to Mexico. I listened respectfully. Folktales always interest me. He told me, too, how King Moctezuma I, five hundred years ago, had sent messengers to the Seven Caves to check on the old traditions, and to visit Coatlicue, the mother of the god Huitzilopochtli, who still dwelled there. And the messengers went, and found the natives of the place were immortals, ageless servants of Coatlicue. The goddess, the snaky lady, lived atop a lofty hill, but Moctezuma's envoys could not climb it, for they sank to their knees in sand and stumbled back. "What is wrong with you, O Aztecs?" the servants of the goddess asked. "What has made you so heavy? What do you eat in your land?" And the envoys told the immortals, "We eat the foods that grow there and we drink chocolatl." The immortals replied, "Such food and drink, my children, have made you heavy and they make it difficult for you to reach the place of your ancestors. Those foods will bring death."

The envoys waited, and the immortals went up the hill to fetch hideous Coatlicue. "Welcome, my sons!" she cried, and the Aztecs presented her with gifts, and told of their plight: they lived only fifty or sixty years, and then died. She told them how her servants change their ages at will; the higher they climb on the hill, the older they become, but when they descend the years drop from them. "We become young when we wish," she said. "You have become old, you have become tired because of the chocolatl you drink and because of the foods you eat. They have harmed and weakened you. You have been spoiled by those mantles, feathers, and riches that you wear. All of that has ruined you."

And the priests sent by Moctezuma as ambassadors wept, for they could not ascend the hill to view the place of their origin. They turned away, and returned to Tenochtitlan.

"It would have been better, perhaps, if we had never left the Seven Caves," said Quequex, taking another swig of the chocolatl and patting his ample waist. "But it could be that it is better to live down here, eat and grow fat and die, than to be ageless upon the hill of Coatlicue. Eh?"

I felt some answer was necessary. I said, "The important thing is to be on the move. To be going somewhere, doing things, seeing, learning, feeling. What's the use of immortality if it has to be spent on the same old hill?"

"You believe this?" he asked.

"I do."

"Good." Quequex leaned forward and jabbed a stubby forefinger deep into my knee. "Remember all your life what you have just said. To reach out—to make voyages—that's what we are human for. I would not ascend Coatlicue's hill, not while

I'm yet to glimpse the shining palaces of Cathay. And you, young Englander far from home—you are on the true path already. Stay to it.''

In the morning, Quequex' mare balked at carrying his load another day. He sold her and bought a new steed, and off we went. The cities were close together now—and they were cities here, not peasant villages—so that we often plodded along in traffic-thick streets. It disturbed me to think that three or four of these Aztec cities had populations greater than London's. Of course, London has more to her than people; she wears two thousand years of history. Caesar trod those streets, and King Arthur, and Harold of Wessex, and James the Valiant, and many another hero unknown to these beak-nosed people of Mexico. Yet today London boasts no more than a hundred thousand citizens. Aztec cities whose names I could scarcely pronounce were twice as populous.

One of the finest of those cities had a name easy on the tongue: Cholula. We entered it by night, when it glowed with the electrical lights that the great cities of the Hesperides have installed, and the sight of it was like a hand reaching within my chest to wrench my heart. I gasped at my first glimpse. Such a city! If this were Cholula, a mere provincial town, what could Tenochtitlan possibly be like?

A religious festival was going on as we arrived. Priests in white cotton surplices paraded, some carrying trumpets, others flutes, other drums. The smell of incense was thick and sweet in the air. Quequex and I rode down the broad thoroughfare following the procession; I was too fascinated even to think of seeking lodging, and he seemed to be willing to humor me in my curiosity.

In the distance I saw a colossal pyramid with more than a hundred steps leading to a temple at the summit. The white-clad priests were ascending the pyramid, and I suspected that we had arrived in time for the climax of the ceremony. In the great square below the pyramid hundreds of thousands of Cholulans had gathered, packed elbow to elbow. I had never seen so many human beings all at once before, and the sight was moderately terrifying: an ocean of bobbing heads, a sea of painted faces.

I whispered, "Are they going to cut out a man's heart up there?"

"There is no human sacrifice at the Great Pyramid of Cholula," Quequex said scornfully.

Notice how the old fox phrased that. He did not claim outright that the Aztecs had given up their bloody ways; he merely denied that such savagery took place here. The official Aztec claim, of course, is that human sacrifice was abolished in the seventeenth century. And, since the Mexicans are a prosperous and civilized lot, I suppose that's basically true. But their gods are blood-drinkers, all the same. It would not surprise me to learn that in the small towns of the back country the old rites still are practiced: the obsidian knives flash, and Huitzilopochtli gets his red offering.

As Quequex explained, this temple was sacred to Quetzalcoatl, an austere god of peace to whom only partridges, doves, and game are sacrificed. He did not out-and-out insist that human sacrifice was extinct. But I was fairly sure that no infidel eyes would ever glimpse such a rite in Mexico, and Quequex wasn't one to talk about those things.

The ceremony ended. The crowd dispersed. We found ourselves lodging in a large hotel, and stabled our horses. Then we went out to walk about Cholula.

It was a sobering experience. The electrical lights dazzled and awed me. Buckingham Palace has electricity now, and so do the Houses of Parliament. But to see an entire city glowing with yellow light after dark—it made me want to sink to my knees in prayer at such wonders! And this, I stress, was a minor city of no more than five hundred thousand people. Temples everywhere, towers, giant statues, an air of wealth and power: that was Cholula. I looked forward almost in fear to my first glimpse of Tenochtitlan.

We left in the morning. Our road was a mountain pass, cold and forbidding, between two snow-covered peaks. There was a tunnel for motorized traffic, but we on horses had to take the ancient road. I was happy that we did, despite the chill that invaded my bones and the thinness of the mountain air. For at midday, fifteen miles or so

out from Cholula, we rounded a bend in the pass
and suddenly there lay out before me on my left
the most awesome mountain I ever expect to see.

"Popocatepetl," said Quequex softly. "The
smoking mountain."

Popo was a stunning cone, his flanks gleaming
with a snowy whiteness so bright it numbed the
eyes, his summit an ashy zone of blackness from
which smoke belched forth. I thought I saw red
flaming tongues licking out of the volcano, too,
but that may have been merely the workings of an
over-stimulated imagination. I reined the black colt
and sat a while in wonder. I had not traveled much
before this journey, you understand. They say that
Switzerland has some fair mountains, but to reach
Switzerland from England one must cross France
or Italy or the Teutonic States, and my patriotic
English blood boils at having to live even a day in
countries that swear yet by the Koran. So I have
forgone the sight of the Alps—not that my family
could ever afford to send its boys around as tourists,
even if I could overcome my religious prejudices.
Once as a lad I vacationed in Wales, and saw
Mount Snowdon, which in its way is a lofty peak.
But Snowdon's way is not the way of Popo, and
beside this towering monster of a volcano the pride
of Wales would be lost.

When my mind had come to terms with the
hugeness of Popocatepetl, Quequex seized my arm
and pointed it toward the right. I narrowed my

eyes, squinting into the noon sun, and saw a second snowcapped mountain far away.

"Ixtaccihuatl," he murmured. "The white woman. The bride of the sun. Popocatepetl is her guardian."

I began to wish I had never come to Mexico. Such wonders are a severe strain on a boy from a small island without great natural splendor. We rode on. Quequex told me tales of the mountains: the rain of ashes and cinders from Popo's cone that in the 1540 eruption had reached Tlaxcla, thirty miles away; the rivers of lava; the rumbling of the earth. We picked our way daintily past the mated volcanoes; I could not help but fear that the drumming of my colt's hooves on the highway would awaken the sleeping giant and bring liquid fire to envelop and destroy.

We spent that night at a place called Huexotzingo. In daylight we ascended another mountain pass, this one so high that it stung the nostrils to draw a breath. Popo and Ixta still lay to the left and to the right, miles away. But a greater sight greeted me that morning, with such an impact that I felt tears bursting from the corners of my eyes at the sight of such a spectacle.

What I saw was Mexico's great lake spread before me, with all its swollen cities along its borders, and Tenochtitlan the proud within the lake itself.

"You see?" Quequex said, pointing. "The big lake is Lake Texcoco. There to the south: Lake

Xochimilco. Adjoining it, toward us: Lake Chalco.
And in the north, barely to be seen: Lake Xaltocan.
All the lakes are joined now. And there, see the
cities!''

His voice trembled, as did his pointing arm. If a
native Mexican could be shaken with emotion upon
seeing such a view, what effect do you think it had
on me? I was speechless. Along the eastern shore
of the vast lake was a continuous band of habitation.
I knew that more people lived about this lake than
in all of England, France, and Spain combined,
but a statement like that is only words, a string of
noises, while the sight before my eyes brought the
meaning of those noises home with stunning force.

Quequex called off the names of cities: Chalco,
Ixtapaluca, Itztahuacan, Chimalhuacan, Coatlinchan,
Huexotla, Texcoco, Tepexpan. I saw only that
unbroken line of buildings, and no hint of borders
between city and city. He named the cities on the
western side of the lake, too, though they were
only graynesses in the haze: Xochimilco, Colhuan-
can, Coyoacan, Mixcoac, Chapultepec, Tlacopan,
and his own native city of Azcapotzalco. The
unending stream of strange syllables cast of hyp-
notic spell, and my head swam with words of x
and z and tl and oa and $ua,$ and at last I snapped
from it and said, ''I have a friend in Texcoco.
When we pass through there, can we visit him?''

''How can you have a friend in Texcoco?''

''Someone I met on the ship coming over.
Nezahualpilli, the son of Ixtlilxochitl.''

"We do not pass through Texcoco on the way to the capital," said Quequex. "See, it is up there, by the widest part of the lake. We go to the south, past Ixtapalapa and Mexicalcingo. But if you wish, we can separate, and you may visit your friend alone. I must go on to Tenochtitlan. I have lingered long enough on this journey, and Moctezuma awaits me."

I hesitated. I wanted to see Nezahualpilli again very badly, to thank him for his gift of money, for that money had sustained me well on my travels so far. (Quequex, as a member of the court, simply charged all his expenses to the royal treasury, but I had to pay my way.) However, I was not eager to part from Quequex, even for the sake of seeing Nezahualpilli. I had come to think of the fat sorcerer as a kind of shabby but beloved uncle, and I wanted to see him safely into the capital. Although I have not seen fit to mention it, we had been set upon several times by bandits during our ride; each time, Quequex' outraged shouts and my willingness to use my knife had driven them off without serious incident, but Quequex' jade necklaces made him a tempting target to those highwaymen who might lie ahead.

Unable to decide what to do, I simply rode onward with Quequex, keeping my eyes fastened to the incredible scene of the lake cities. We came down out of the pass and rode to Amecameca, a city of the province of Chalco, with a population of perhaps a hundred thousand—a London-sized city, though of no great note here. And as we trotted through rich plantations of cacao on the far side of Amecameca, my dilemma solved itself when a deep voice cried out:

"Dan! Dan Beauchamp!"

I swung around so fast I nearly fell from my colt. Who knew my name, in this Hesperidean hemisphere? Who but Nezahualpilli?

He stood knee-deep in weeds beside a cacao tree bristling with red wrinkled pods, a machete in his hand. I had not recognized him among his workmen, for he wore no more than they did: a bit of white cloth twisted round the hips. He tossed his chopper away and came towards me as I dismounted. I saw then the marks of aristocracy: the jeweled plugs inserted in his earlobes, the jade pendant on his chest. He had been working hard; his whole lean body was oiled with sweat, and his bare skin was mirror-bright. His shoulder-length black hair was caught up by a jade circlet in back, dangling down in a pony-tail style.

"I was on my way to Texcoco to visit you," I said. It was a lie, but a small one. "What are you doing down here?"

"I have been here eight days now. My marriage has been celebrated. These are my wife's plantations. After her father dies they will be mine."

He swept his hand around to indicate a vast area. I saw cacao trees everywhere, on both sides of the road, growing amidst the taller trees that are necessary to shade them. I began to understand why Nezahualpilli's father had made this match for him.

I introduced him to Quequex, Quequex to him. They both seemed awed, Quequex because my friend was a rich man, Nezahualpilli because I was traveling in the company of a sorcerer to the court. They eyed one another warily.

Then Nezahualpilli said, "Come! I will declare a holiday, and you are my guests!"

He led us to the plantation house. I had never been inside a Mexican home before, only hotels and roadside hostelries. Of course, this place was hardly typical: a cool palace of white-washed mud walls, arranged in a rectangular design around a central courtyard. The rooms were richly furnished, and—a sign of great wealth—electrical lights were burning in most of them, even in the daytime.

"This is my wife," Nezahualpilli said. "Her name is Atotoztli."

My heart went out to him.

Atotoztli is a lovely name, as Aztec names go, but her loveliness ended there. She was squat, dark-skinned, and thick-bodied, with a prominent mustache. If the eyes are the windows of the soul, Atotoztli's soul did not get much of a view, for her lids drooped in a sure sign of stupidity. She smiled at us, the shy, hopeful smile of a dull, unattractive woman who knows her own disadvantages. Nezahualpilli looked pained as he presented her. But this was his wife, and this was the Aztec system, and now he was as rich as a duke. After a decent interval, though, he could add a second wife more to his liking.

Atotoztli vanished into the maze of rooms that was the house, and we never saw her again, which is just as well. As in any warrior society, the wives kept well to the background. We settled on mats and slaves brought us bowls of cold chocolatl, and trays heaped high with food, including fresh fruit nestling on mounds of ice.

I thanked Nezahualpilli for his gift. He laughed. "As you can see, it is nothing. Don't embarrass me by mentioning it again."

Quequex asked him a few things about his family. It turned out that Quequex and Nezahualpilli's father had met at court, some years ago, and they talked about that for a while. The feast went on and on. I said very little, once I had described my journey from the coast.

Hours later, I found myself alone with Nezahualpilli for the first time. He said to me, "The man you want to see is named Topiltzin."

I was puzzled. "What man? Where?"

"Aboard the ship, you told me you wished to find a place for yourself in Mexico. I advised you to seek out an ambitious young prince and pledge your allegiance to him."

"Yes," I said. "And then when I asked you for the name of such a man, you refused to answer. You said you weren't from Tenochtitlan and didn't know such things."

"That is true. But since my return to Mexico I

have asked some questions. I have been told of a man with whom you might be well rewarded. He is Prince Topiltzin.''

''Who is he?''

''The son of King Moctezuma's youngest brother. He is our age, restless, energetic, full of plans. I am told that he is in great trouble with his own family, and wishes to go far away and found his empire. He may come to nothing; but he may achieve much.''

My heart beat a little faster. ''Where can he be found?''

''He lives in Tenochtitlan. Not at the court, for he is in disgrace. This man you are traveling with can help you find him. This Quequex—he knows everyone and everything. Wait until you are in the city, then ask.''

''Topiltzin,'' I said, savoring the name.

''Topiltzin, yes. Do you know the name's history? A thousand years ago, when the Toltec nation ruled Mexico, before the Aztecs came, Topiltzin was the Toltec king. He sought to do away with human sacrifice and the worship of the death-god. His people drove him away and he sailed into the east. The legend of Quetzalcoatl is based on Topiltzin's story.''

''A bold name.''

''And a bold namesake,'' said Nezahualpilli.

We spent a joyous night of feasting at Nezahualpilli's estate. I regret to say that the intoxicating liquors flowed rather freely, so that when I woke

in the morning my head throbbed and I felt it most
unlikely that I would ever live to see my nineteenth birthday. Chocolatl, that wondrous stuff,
revived me. Before we left, Nezahualpilli pressed
a parting gift on me: a ring of gold, inlaid with
turquoises. In England, such a ring would be worn
only by a prince of the royal family, and I gasped
at its beauty and magnificence. It was useless to
protest the gift, of course. I slipped the ring on my
finger and felt as puffed-up as though His Majesty
King Richard had just proclaimed me Daniel, First
Duke of Beauchamp. I bade my friend farewell.
He wished me all luck when I met Topiltzin.

And then it was onward for Quequex and me.

We were in the suburbs, now, and the towns
streamed by, one flowing into the next. Each little
district had its own name, which I'll not bother to
record here. Soon we were at the lake. We passed
through Ixtapalapa and jogged out onto the causeway that led to Tenochtitlan.

Once, centuries ago, Tenochtitlan had been a
small island in a watery bulge toward the western
part of Lake Texcoco. Now the city had spread.
They had filled in the land, so that the capital
reached some five miles to the east of its old
boundary. But for partly superstitious reasons they
had kept it an island. Now a narrow strip of water
bounded Tenochtitlan on three sides, and a somewhat greater strip on the fourth, and causeways led
over to the sprawling mainland suburbs. Each of
these causeways contained a drawbridge so that in

time of attack Tenochtitlan could be isolated. But
who would dare to attack Tenochtitlan the proud?

At the end of the causeway was a gate, topped
by a huge tower at either side, and a crenelated
battlement linking the towers. The gate was open,
but pompous guards in medieval dress flanked it,
spears in hand. The traffic sped right past those
gentlemen and into the city, and we entered it
slightly past midday, in the month of October,
1985, some two months after I had left London.

I was in Tenochtitlan, the world's greatest city.

How can I describe it to you? What words can I
possibly use to speak of a city of nine million
people? There are not nine million people in all of
Britain. The best pens of the world have tried in
vain to capture the essence of this king among
cities. What can I do, when the masters have
failed?

Let me try.

Quequex wisely let me explore the city for most
of the afternoon, without a word of dispute, never
once suggesting that he would like to leave me and
go about his business. He rode with me, and a
good thing, for had I been left alone in Tenochtitlan I would have dropped to my knees, paralyzed
with awe, and remained there for weeks.

The city has a medieval air. They have pre-
served the heart of the ancient Aztec capital, temples and pyramids and palaces and all, and about it
have risen the monumental buildings of a modern
commercial city. Some of the office buildings in

Tenochtitlan are fifteen and twenty stories high, and seem to scrape at the heavens. Their walls are richly inlaid with shining stones, and when these towers are in the full light of the sun they make one cover one's eyes against the glare.

The tall buildings were impressive enough. But it was the old city in which I wandered that first day. And here I fall short of words.

The city of a living god, Moctezuma the Twelfth, the city of cities. Here was Moctezuma's palace, beautiful beyond any telling of it, and about it the lesser palaces of his royal ancestors. Near it the *teocalli*, that is to say the temple, a double pyramid a hundred feet high dedicated to the gods Huitzilopochtli and Tlaloc. Its twin stairways were stained dark crimson. I knew the tale: 80,000 prisoners of war had been sacrificed by King Ahuitzotl, half a thousand years ago, to consecrate this temple. Uncounted legions had lost their hearts on its summit in the two hundred years before the rite of sacrifice was abolished. The rains of centuries would not rinse away that devilish stain.

The temple site was a vast plaza, enclosed by mighty walls broken by four gates. The pyramid itself was terraced, and I saw the altars at the top, and shivered. Between those altars priests once had stood, stooping forward to pluck out throbbing hearts, working in deadly rhythm, cutting, grasping, holding aloft, cutting, grasping, holding aloft.

And the lesser teocallis, large and small, forty or fifty of them, temples of Tezcatlipoca and Xipe

Totec and Quetzalcoatl and Coatlicue and more gods than my mind could cope with. And the great marketplaces, close by the temple, where all the treasures of an empire were traded, cacao and cotton cloaks, gold and silver, jade, turquoise, the feathers of marvelous birds, copper tools, the seeds of chocolatl, the aromatic weed tobacco, pottery, and of course slaves, since the Aztecs deal in the souls of men.

I was dazzled. My glorious London shriveled in my memory, for London is a small town, and Tenochtitlan is the city of cities. I was sick with envy and amazement.

Quequex, beside me, murmured a poem:

"The city is spread out in circles of jade,
Radiating flashes of light like quetzal plumes.
Beside it the lords are borne in boats.
Over them extends a flowery mist."

And it was so. Do you know the bird, the quetzal? Its shining feathers have all the hues of the rainbow. Tenochtitlan glowed in quetzal colors. Narrow canals sliced up the city, so that it looked as I imagine that shameful but lovely Moslem town of Venice looks. Down these canals came handsome nobles, lolling in long, narrow boats while sweating slaves poled them along. Was one of those perfumed dandies my Topiltzin? It could be. They all seemed like the sons of kings.

And the processions, through the streets: aristocrats in flowery litters, dimly visible, haughtily staring outward. Lovely ladies enmeshed in jade beads, preceded by bearers armed with feather-tipped poles; the poles swung, the feathers brushed across eyelids, and the lady passed unseen. This was a barbaric city. I looked for the mound of skulls, said to be as tall as the temple pyramid itself, but Quequex told me it had been taken away long ago.

Tenochtitlan the proud! I had journeyed so long from London that my goal had become unreal, and it was as though I lived now in a city of dreams. Quequex told me of the palace of Moctezuma, with its house of feathers, inhabited by living birds of every known species, a symphony of plumage; and he spoke of the garden of the animals, with its jaguars and lions and giraffes; and he told of the garden of aromatic herbs, and of the golden dishes on which the King ate, and of the company of six hundred noblemen that waited table for him, and so many more tales of luxury that I begged him to be silent, for he was causing my brain to spin.

We went down crowded streets barely wide enough to admit our horses. We paused at vendors' stands, and Quequex bought me fruits I had never seen before, of several different colors, so sweet and juicy that they seemed sinful to eat. He took me to the marketplace, aflame with mother-of-pearl and chalcedony, emeralds and amethysts, all these precious stones changing possession swiftly, their purchasers heedless of the cost. Such wealth! Such throngs! Such color and vividness!

There is an intoxication of excitement that is far more powerful than any intoxication that comes from a bottle. Such an intoxication I suffered that day in Tenochtitlan. I had dreamed a Tenochtitlan of my own, put together from books and pictures, and the reality was infinitely more amazing.

"I am weary," I told Quequex. "I am exhausted. I need to rest." And he took me to a place where I might rest.

SIX

TOPILTZIN

We sold our horses in the marketplace, taking a small loss, and Quequex conducted me by hired boat, up one canal and down the next, until we reached a small, shabby hotel. I was grateful for the shabbiness, and for the dowdiness of the surrounding neighborhood. If I had spent another hour amid the glitter of central Tenochtitlan I would have died of overwhelming awe, but there was nothing overwhelming about this quarter.

When I was safely ensconced in the hotel Quequex said, "I am grateful for your company on this journey, my friend. Three times at least you have saved my life, and I am grateful three times over." Abruptly he lifted one of the heaviest of the jade necklaces from himself and draped it

over my shoulders. There were some fifty tapering
slabs of the polished green stone, weighing several
pounds in all; I sagged a bit beneath it. I began to
protest the gift, and he shut me up. I protested no
more. I was beginning to learn how to accept
lavish gifts gracefully.

It occurred to me that Quequex' jade and Nezahualpilli's ring gave me considerable capital. I
could sell such things at a high price, even assum-
ing I'd be cheated somewhat, and on the proceeds
I'd be able to last for several years. On the other
hand, these treasures made me vulnerable to bandits,
and I was more grateful than ever for the journey's
humblest gift, Opothle's keen knife.

"I can repay you for your services in one other
way," said Quequex. I wanted to tell him that
there was no need for any repayment, that he had
been as useful to me as I to him, but he swept on,
saying, "I can present you at court. Would you
find it interesting to meet the King? Four days
from now I can get you an audience with Moctezuma. In our calendar, today is the day Three
Eagle. On Seven Eagle you will go to the royal
palace and touch the King's hand. Yes?"

"It's too much," I said. "I'd be afraid. The
King himself—"

"—is only a man, like the rest of us. He will
not eat you. You will have a rare opportunity to
see the interior of the palace. Will you be there?"

"Yes," I said.

And I was so dazed at the thought of shaking

hands with Moctezuma that I nearly forgot to ask the question I had been saving for this moment. Quequex bade me farewell and waddled from the room, and just as the door closed I shrieked his name. He came back in, looking surprised.

"I have something to ask you," I told him. "There's a prince named Topiltzin—do you know him?"

Quequex' face went cold as death. His eyes slitted until only a white gleam was visible. He said slowly, "I know him, yes. What of him?"

"Where can I find him?"

"You do not want to find him."

"It's important that I see him."

"Topiltzin is a very dangerous man, friend Dan. He has the touch of the grave about him. His company you do not need to keep."

"Nevertheless, I have to talk to him."

Quequex sighed. "Who put this idea in your head? Your tall friend Nezahualpilli, it must have been. He's the only one. Take my advice; forget Topiltzin. He is in disfavor here. One day Moctezuma might strike off his head. If you happened to be around, your head would roll too."

"I'm a good guardian of my neck, Quequex. I ask this as a personal favor; help me find Topiltzin. A man with your connections won't have any difficulty tracking him down."

"A personal favor, you say?"

"A personal favor."

There was a long silence. Quequex tugged at his

chins, fiddled with his earplugs of jade. At length
he said, "I am indebted to you for my life, three
times over. I cannot refuse such a request."

I waited.

"But Topiltzin is an evil rascal. If I send you to
him, I may be sending you to your death."

"I'll chance it," I said. "Will you find him for
me?"

"I will find him for you," said Quequex.

For the next two days I was on my own. I ate at
the hotel that night, and rested soundly, and in the
morning, on the day of Four Eagle, I went back
into central Tenochtitlan feeling not quite so stunned
by it all. I roamed about like any sightseer, doing
the public buildings, the temples and lesser palaces.
I spent a long time in the marketplace. As I
expected, no one approached me. In a city this
size, every man is a stranger and the barriers are
never breached.

I wondered about Quequex' warnings. Did he
have some personal dislike for Topiltzin? Or was
he genuinely concerned that I wanted anything to
do with him? He hadn't pressed me for information,
but he had left me with the idea that Topiltzin was
an idler, a wastrel, a man of no account. Quequex
seemed eager to protect me from falling into his
clutches, and Quequex was a good friend with no
motive to injure me. On the other hand, Nezahualpilli was a good friend, too, and it was he that had
given me Topiltzin's name.

Time would tell. I would see this Topiltzin, and make up my own mind about him.

On Five Eagle, I played the part of a tourist once again. Of course, I could stroll through Tenochtitlan for the rest of my life and never see it all, but this time I covered a good deal in the western part of the city, crossing the bridge onto the mainland and inspecting the sacred hill at Chapultepec.

When I returned to the hotel, there was a message waiting for me from Quequex.

I tugged open the sealed sheet of thick paper and found that he had written Topiltzin's address—and he had written it in English. Thoughtful of him, I told myself. He realizes that I can't read the Aztec alphabet as well as I can speak the Aztec language. But then it occurred to me that he might have had a less considerate reason; if Topiltzin's address happens to be a deep secret to the local authorities, Quequex was taking the route of caution by writing it down in a script few people here understood.

At the hotel office I inquired about the location of such-and-such a street, and was pleasantly surprised to learn that it was only a short journey from where I was. At the nearest canal I hired a boat, and within half an hour I was on the street where Topiltzin lived.

I found the house easily enough. It must have been a grand palace in the days of early Aztec glory, but somewhere along the line it had been

subdivided and now was a cheap boarding house
badly in need of repainting. It seemed improbable
to me that a prince of the royal blood would spend
so much as six minutes in a place like that. But
Topiltzin, I reflected, had come upon hard times.

I went in.

According to Quequex' message, Topiltzin occupied an apartment on the ground floor. I knew no
more than that. I picked a direction at random—
the left—and walked down the narrow, musty-
smelling hallway. There were doors. Which was
Topiltzin's? Did I knock at each until I found the
right one?

I stood in the half-darkness, baffled a moment.

Then hands slid under my arms from behind.
They came up across my chest and locked around
my throat. I made a gurgling sound and the hands
dug in tightly.

"Go it silent, now," muttered the deepest bass
voice I had ever heard. "What do you want here?"

I couldn't answer, because my windpipe was in
the grip of those steely fingers. My lungs cried out
for air; my knees sagged. I toyed with the idea of
reaching for my knife and rapidly swinging my
arm back to drive the blade into my captor's side.
But the instant I twitched a muscle in my arm the
fingers pressed more brutally.

Consciousness started to ebb.

"You have no business here," the unknown as-
sailant said in that midnight voice. "You regret

coming here already, don't you? You wish you'd stayed away.''

My legs buckled. I dropped toward the floor, half feigning a faint and half fainting for true. I fell so leadenly that the hands on my throat relaxed their grip.

That was the opportunity I wanted.

I gulped air deep into my aching lungs. Then I swung around, seized my attacker's left ankle, and yanked hard. He came crashing to the floor, doubtless surprised to get pulled over by a man he had just choked into unconsciousness. I got my first clear look at him as he landed beside me. He was an African, the blackest man imaginable, the color of his skin so deep that it looked purple. He must have been about thirty. His close-cropped woolly hair rode high on his shining forehead; his body was compact and powerful, with enormously wide shoulders; muscles rippled like cords on his bare arms.

Before he could seize me again, I jumped on him and tried to smash his skull against the floor. He didn't smash so easily. I gripped his shoulders and forced him down with all my strength, but he levered himself up, inch by inch. Veins stood out on his dark forehead. My muscles quivered and red streaks blazed in my brain as I pushed him toward the floor again. I got him about six inches from the floor, and there he stuck, my knees pinning his arms, my hands gripping his shoulders. His eyes were bright and wide, and he was grinning despite his effort, displaying a double row of large gleaming teeth.

Down—down—down—

But it was clear to me that I couldn't get his head all the way down. He was too strong. I could choke him, though, and try not to make the mistake that he had made with me. My hands slid inward from his shoulders to his collarbone and I began applying pressure to his throat.

Slowly he weakened and grew limp. It was a fantastic struggle, but I was winning it. I didn't want to choke him. I respected his enormous strength, in a way. But he had attacked me. He had grabbed me from the rear. And if I had to choke him to unconsciousness to save myself, why, I'd do it.

He wasn't grinning now. He was grimacing in pain. Another moment—

And then I felt what could only be the tip of a spear prod none too tenderly into my back.

"Release him," said a man with a high, feathery voice. "Release him and stand up. Put your hands high over your head. Now!"

The cold metal dug a little deeper into me. I released the African, rolled free of him, and got to my feet, with my hands overhead. The African, looking a bit the worse for wear, sprang up and pulled my knife from its sheath. Then the man with the spear came around to face me.

He was a native of the Hesperides, but he wasn't a Mexican. His clothing was different and his appearance was different. His skin was darker, his cheekbones less prominent, his nose rounded instead of sharp. I suppose he was about twenty-five years old. He held the spear as though he would gladly plunge it deep into my chest if I made a false move.

"Why are you here?" he asked me.

"To see Topiltzin."

"Who is Topiltzin?"

"The son of the King's brother. He lives here. You know that as well as I do."

"There is no Topiltzin here."

"Then who are you? Why did you jump me?"

"We did not know your business. You are a stranger. You may be dangerous."

I eyed the tip of the spear, not very far from my waist. "Will you stop this nonsense and take me to Topiltzin?"

"We do not know a Topiltzin."

"You're lying!"

"Why do you think Topiltzin is here?"

"I know he's here," I said.

"How can you know it?"

"I was told."

"By whom?"

I hesitated. "By Quequex the sorcerer."

A moment of silence. The black man and the spearholder exchanged glances. They said something in a language I did not understand.

Then he of the spear said to me, "What business do you have with Topiltzin?"

"I want to serve him. To fight for him. I'm looking for adventure."

Another conference. Then:

"Turn around. Keep your hands above your head. Walk straight forward."

I was taken to the presence of Topiltzin.

They marched me down that musty hall to a distant doorway, where I halted while the African opened a latch. We entered. Within, in a battered, dilapidated apartment, draperies and cloths had been hung to provide a semblance of Aztec opulence, and in the middle of the floor, reclining comfortably on a thick mat, was Topiltzin.

He looked somewhat like Nezahualpilli: long-legged, as many of these Aztecs are, with shoulder-length jet-black hair, sleek swarthy skin, a lean, muscular frame. His nose was long, his lips were thin, his eyes were dark and sly. He got lazily to his feet, curling up from the mat as though he had no bones at all, and eyed me with that fishy stare practiced by aristocrats all over the world.

"Well. What are you?" he said.

I despised him at that moment. He had said only four words, yet I decided at once that he was vain, arrogant, lazy, supercilious, and cruel. In truth he really was all those things, but there were strengths in Topiltzin that I did not learn till later. At first glance he seemed foppish.

I said, "I am an Englishman, come to your country to find excitement and adventure. I'm looking for military service with a likely prince. Your name was given to me.''

''By whom?''

''A friend,'' I said, unwilling to get Nezahualpilli involved too deeply in this.

''By Quequex,'' said the African.

''Quequex is no friend of mine,'' Topiltzin declared.

I said, ''He is a friend of mine. But it was another who told me to seek you out. Quequex merely located you for me. Against his will, I might add. He does not think highly of you.''

''As well he might not,'' said Topiltzin. He laughed. ''Quequex was at court when I disgraced myself last. Do you know what I did, yellow-haired stranger? I took my cousin Chimalpopoca, the favorite son of my uncle the King, and fed him on liquor until he could not tell up from down. And then he burst into the throne room when Moctezuma was with his council, and did shameful things before them all.'' Topiltzin laughed at the recollection. ''Later he implicated me, and I was in trouble again. But it was worth the consequences. To see that stuffy little boy turning handsprings in the councilroom—!''

''And you are in disfavor for a small thing like that?''

''No, stranger. For many things of which that was but the last and the least.'' He walked over to me. He was a head taller than I, and I had to crane my neck to peer into his cold black eyes. "What are you looking for in Mexico, Englishman?"

"Land. Fortune. A name among warriors."

"Have you fought in war?"

"Only in my dreams."

"Have you killed?"

"I could kill, if the need arose."

"But you have taken no lives?"

"No."

"Can you fight?"

"Ask your African friend," I said.

Topiltzin looked at the black man. The black man expressively touched his throat.

"He can fight," he said.

"Will you follow me anywhere?"

"Anywhere, Prince. So long as a reward lies at the end of the journey."

Topiltzin smiled. Then, without warning, his foot lashed out and swept behind my right heel. He hooked my heel in such a way that my leg went out from under me. I began to fall forward, and in the same instant his long arms reached out to seize my head and shoulders. His aim, I think, was to grasp me and hurl me in an arc against the wall.

I moved so swiftly I surprised myself. As I swayed toward him, I slapped my right foot against the floor to steady my body, and at the same moment I slipped under Topiltzin's grasping hands and caught him by the throat. I flexed my knees, straightened them again, and heaved. The prince flew gracefully through the air and landed in a tangle of limbs on his couch.

Instantly the African had my own knife against my ribs and the other was menacing me with his spear. Topiltzin rose slowly, rearranging his jade bangles a bit, and gestured to them. "Back," he said. "Let him be. That was well done, Englishman. Your name?"

"Dan Beauchamp."

"Which is the first name?"

"Dan."

"It happens, Dan, that we are about to leave on a mission of enterprise. There might be a place for you. I have not often been thrown to the ground in such a way."

"I meant no offense, Prince. It was sheer self defense."

"Of course. I tested you, and you passed the test. I shall impose only one more test on you."

"I stand ready."

"Tomorrow at midday," Topiltzin said, "you will come with us to the ball courts. Are you skilled at tlachtli?"

"It is a game I've never played."

"One learns the rules fast. Play tlachtli with us. That will be your final test."

It was arranged that the three of them would call for me at my hotel tomorrow morning and go with me to the ball courts, which were not far from the temple precincts. I was uneasy, for I had heard grim things of the Mexican national sport, but there was no backing out now.

Topiltzin introduced me to his two comrades before I left. The black man was Sagaman Musa of the Mali Empire. I took back my knife from him. The spearwielder was a Peruvian, Manco Huascar, who according to Topiltzin was an exile member of the royal family of the Incas. Evidently Topiltzin was collecting the restless riffraff of all nations for his planned adventure.

I was restless too. And I suppose I could be considered riffraff. A pity I couldn't lay claim to being a banished scion of the House of Plantagenet, perhaps second cousin to King Richard. But Topiltzin would have to make do with me as I was. Common blood or not, I could fight, as I had demonstrated amply today. If only I lived through that ball game, I knew I would have a place on Topiltzin's staff.

SEVEN

WE PLAY A LITTLE GAME

I KNEW something of this Aztec sport already. On my journey to Tenochtitlan from the coast, I had stopped with Quequex in a city that had a fair-sized stadium. We had watched the ruffians play a while, and then, after the game had ended, we went down into the ball court itself, for Quequex wished to show me some handsome bas-reliefs along the walls. I saw sculptured scenes of lively action, depicting the players at their game. And toward the end of the field I saw one bas-relief that did not duplicate anything I had witnessed. The death-god, Tezcatlipoca, all bones and skull, presided over a ceremony in which the captain of the losing team was being sacrificed by the victors. A flint knife had been plunged into his chest, while the players, still in their uniforms, stood by and watched.

"In the old days," Quequex had said, "it was not uncommon to put an entire team to death if it lost."

I shivered. "Why would anyone want to play such a game, considering the risks?"

"Not to play," said Quequex, "was not to be a man."

And even today the game seemed to be the ultimate test of manhood. It pleased me to know that the losers no longer paid for their athletic shortcomings with their lives. But from what I had seen and what I knew in advance, I was expecting a rugged time. I was not disappointed.

Topiltzin, Sagaman Musa, and Manco Huascar came to get me early the next day. I had slept poorly. Since Topiltzin was supposedly in hiding, I didn't understand how he would dare to make an appearance in so public a place as the grand tlachtli court, but when he showed up I saw the answer. He was in disguise. A thin rubber mask over his face was enough to conceal his identity.

I unslung my knife and started to take off the gold ring Nezahualpilli had given me, figuring that they'd be in the way during the game. But Manco Huascar shook his head. "Take those things with you. You'll have need of them."

We went downtown.

Evidently this game had already been scheduled, for a goodly crowd had gathered to watch it. I felt

small and insignificant as I stepped into the stadium.
It was of colossal size, possibly 500 feet long and
150 feet wide. From the middle of each of the long
walls projected a stone ring, mounted vertically
about twenty feet overhead. Benches rose in tiers
above these goals, and there was room for thousands of spectators.

Knots of players were huddled at the far end of
the field. They were wearing thick leather belts
that covered them from chest to waist, with leather
armshields as well, and leather gloves. Legs and
shoulders were bare. Topiltzin led the way toward
the group.

As I approached, I saw a heap of treasure on the
ground at one side of the court—a mound of ear
plugs, pendants, anklets, golden beads, and other
costly items. Sagaman Musa said to me, "It is the
wager. Each player must add to the stakes. The
winning team divides the booty."

Topiltzin shed the magnificent feather cloak he
was wearing and dropped it on the pile. He added
his jade ear plugs and a pouch of jingling golden
beads. Manco Huascar put down a turquoise necklace and a superb cloth cape of the Peruvian weave.
Sagaman Musa put down nothing. Everyone looked
at me.

What could I give?

Reluctantly I pulled Nezahualpilli's ring from
my finger and tossed it on the treasure-mound. I
waited, hoping to be told that that was sufficient.

"More," said a squat, burly Aztec who turned out to be the captain of the other team.

My hand shook a little as I removed Opothle's knife and added it to the heap. Now we *had* to win, I told myself, or I'd be weaponless in Mexico. The squat one seemed satisfied; perhaps he realized that I had nothing left to give. Quequex' jade necklace was back in my hotel room.

"Come," said Topiltzin. "You must get dressed now."

He took me to a room below the stadium, where slaves quickly stripped off my clothing and covered my entire body with a pungent spicy perfumed oil. Then I was given a white cloth tunic to wrap about my hips. Over it went the massive leather belt. It was six inches thick, and must have weighed thirty pounds. I slipped on the arm-shields, which protected me from wrist to shoulder, and the gloves. For my head I wore a leather helmet. Topiltzin and Manco Huascar were similarly attired. Sagaman Musa, though, remained in street clothes.

"What about you?" I asked.

The African smiled broadly. "I do not play this game. It is much too dangerous for a man of my limited strength."

I had to laugh at that, remembering the wrestling match I had had with the powerful Malian. He was having his little joke. Evidently he did not feel the need to prove his manhood on this playing field.

We stepped into the open again.

The teams were unequal in size, which did not seem to matter. We had thirteen men, they had fifteen. Since one of our men—me—had never played this game before, the odds seemed all the more unequal. I said a silent farewell to Nezahualpilli's ring and Opothle's keen blade.

Topiltzin said, "You know the game?"

"We have to knock a ball through one of those rings."

"Right. The ring on that side is ours. Remember that. Once it happened that in the heat of play a man grew confused and scored a goal for the other team. His teammates trampled him to death on the field in their anger."

"How long does the game last?"

"Until one side scores. It is not easy to score."

"And how long does that take, on the average?"

"There was a game that ended a moment after it had begun," said Topiltzin. "There was another that was played for three days, stopping only when darkness fell, until it was decided. But usually the games last several hours."

"And what are the rules?"

"You must never touch the ball with your hand. It is permissible to kick it, to butt it, to push it. You may inflict any injury you can upon members of the other team, for we must keep them from preventing us from scoring. Those are the rules."

A free-for-all, in other words.

I looked up at the audience. I saw mounds of jewelry and cloaks up there, too: the spectators were placing side-bets. The betting activity seemed fierce. It seemed odd to me that such an important event could be entered by a perfect stranger, and that the sides could be unequal; there was a strangely informal way about the organization of this game, as if youngsters on a street had merely chosen up sides. But yet huge sums were being wagered, both by the players and the spectators.

The game was about to begin. Our fifteen opponents were lined up at the far end of the court, more than 500 feet away. We stood along a baseline facing them. I was to Topiltzin's left, Manco Huascar to his right. I knew none of the other players, nor had they been introduced to me.

A figure rose in what looked like a royal box, jutting out over the center of the playing field. Topiltzin whispered, "It is Axayacatl, my cousin, the King's son, who is to be king one day. He would have my skin if he knew I was here."

I stared at the stocky, commanding figure. The Crown Prince seemed to be a man in his late thirties, extremely regal in appearance. In his hand he held a rubber ball about six inches in diameter. He hurled it high into the air.

The players charged from both sides of the field.

Running forward was a strain I had not expected. Tenochtitlan, like all of central Mexico, is elevated far above sea level, and the air is thin. It does not nourish the lungs. Then, too, I was weighed down by that huge belt. The others were, too, but they were accustomed to it. So I was one of the last to reach the melee in the center of the court.

The ball had bounced twenty feet high when it hit the ground, had bounced again, and then had been seized by two members of the opposition. Our side roared toward them. It was illegal to touch the ball with your hands, perhaps, bert nothing was said about using your hands on a rival player. I saw Manco Huascar smash his fists into the face of an opponent, two at a time, *boom*. The man fell down, spitting out teeth. While I was admiring that, someone caught me from behind and gave me a spin that sent me sprawling to the ground, and someone else jumped on my back with his bare feet, leaving me gasping and retching. I managed to get up, and punched him in the chest just above his leather yoke. He staggered back, but did not fall.

The crowd screamed in sudden excitement.

I whirled around and discovered that in the confusion three of the players of the other side had gained control of the ball. Two of them were forming a human fence, batting away our men as they charged, and the third was taking dead aim on his goal! He kicked, scooping the ball from the ground with a deft sidewise stroke, and I watched in horror as the rubber globe soared on a steep angle toward the stone ring high above us. Was this to be one of the games that ended in the first minute? All action on the field was suspended.

The ball hit the ring and bounced harmlessly away.

I saw it heading straight for me. Imitating Manco Huascar, I shoved both of my fists into the face of the nearest opponent and pounced on the ball.

Topiltzin yelled to me to kick it to him. He was halfway across the field, heading for our goal.

Now, we have a game in England called soccer, which is not too different from this Aztec sport. There, too, one must not touch the ball with one's hands. It happens that I have played some soccer, and am fairly skillful at getting the ball around the field. Just as Topiltzin called to me, two players rushed toward me with murder in their eyes, and I left them gaping and baffled by a little fast footwork. With short, controlled kicks I carried the ball around them, then cut loose with a harsh smash that sent it fifty feet across the ground to Topiltzin. He had time only to kick it in the general direction of the goal before a monstrous Aztec flattened him with a powerful thrust. Manco Huascar, near the goal, gained the ball, kicked it toward the stone ring, but he was too close and it was an impossible angle.

A moment later I nearly scored the winning goal.

The ball bounced back from our ring, and an opponent knocked it all the way across to his side of the field. It was intercepted there by two of our men, who kicked it halfway back. There, one of them let fly with a potent smash intended to be a

pass. The ball came straight at my head at a
fantastic speed and bounced off my helmet. I
staggered, dizzy for the moment, dimly aware that
the crowd was screaming.

Then I looked up. The ball had ricocheted from
my thick skull and was on its way toward the goal!

Another six inches and we'd have won then and
there. But the ball skittered away. Topiltzin laughed
and slapped me on the back.

"A pity your aim wasn't better," he said.

Three times in the first ten minutes of the game
there had been attempts to score, including my
unintentional one. But it was fifteen minutes before anyone was in a position to try again. Back
and forth we raged across the field, kicking the
ball and each other, neither team maintaining possession long enough to achieve anything.

There was no such thing as time out to catch
breath. There were no quarters, no halves in this
game; the idea was to play until you dropped, it
seemed. By the time the game was half an hour
old I was moving like a machine, numb in every
limb, simply cruising the field on sheer stubbornness. I had been hit hard more times than I could
count, but I had done my share of hitting, too.

And I felt a trifle contemptuous of my fellow
players on both sides. Considering that the Aztecs
had been playing this game since the fourteenth
century, they had developed remarkably little in
the way of tactics. Except for the most basic
formations, they knew no teamwork. It was incon-

ceivable for six or seven men to form a flying wedge, for instance, that would carry the ball across the field. Nor did they know much about moving the ball with their feet. They simply bashed away at it, kicking, occasionally slamming it with their hips, giving it a ride with a knee. Their idea of the game was to kick hard and fight hard and trust to luck to get the ball through the hoop. No wonder the games lasted three days before anyone scored!

I made the error of showing off.

Soccer had always been one of my favorite sports. I gave them a bit of my soccer technique here. After one scrambling melee, the ball came spurting out of a heap of flesh down near the south end of the field, and I went for it. I got it and kicked it back up toward the goal area, playing it from one foot to the other until some opponents made for me. Then I got fancy. I nudged the ball with my toe and let it slide up my leg to my knee, and kicked it a little way into the air, just so I could reach it with my forehead. Then I began to dribble the ball, clubbing it hard with my head and maintaining a tight control over each bounce.

The crowd began to bellow and the players on both sides gaped in stupefaction as I did my little trick. As though moving through rows of sleep-walkers I dribbled around them and headed for the goal. Manco Huascar appeared from somewhere and I passed the ball to him, for the Inca obviously knew more about the difficult business of kicking to the goal than I did. Manco kicked. He missed.

And then the whole opposition team came toward me at once.

On the plains of the Upper Hesperides they have a big woolly brown kind of cattle called bison, which travel in herds of several million. I have seen the bison herds on the run, and they make a sound like thunder in the earth, but a million bison are as nothing compared with fifteen angry Aztecs intent on slaughter. As one man, they had decided that the white-skinned foreigner knew too many funny stunts. They were going to eliminate me then and there.

They rumbled over me like angry bison, and I thought I was going to die. Honestly. I was at the bottom of a heap of fists and knees. My teammates had piled on, too, trying to get me away, and the result was that just about everyone was on me. I later learned that Topiltzin had shrewdly taken advantage of the incident to corral the ball and kick a few shots at the goal unmolested, but he didn't succeed.

In soccer, we have umpires to prevent the worst bloodshed. There were no umpires here. The fight went on until someone noticed what Topiltzin was doing, and then they headed for him. I crawled out, dazed and enfeebled. There was blood all over me, much of it mine, and though none of my bones seemed broken a good many of them appeared severely bent.

I was not about to jump right back into the game, and let anyone who wishes make derogatory remarks about my manhood. On hands and knees I crept to the sidelines and sat there, gasping for breath, waiting for my head to stop ticking.

That made the lineup twelve men against fifteen, but I couldn't help it. For five minutes or so I sat there, watching the other twenty-seven doing their best to ruin one another. During that time the odds were evened considerably. A long, lean member of the other team was taking aim on the goal when Manco Huascar came up behind him, calmly lifted both arms high over his head, and brought them down, elbows first, on the player's skull. The man folded instantly and lay like a corpse on the field for a few minutes, until one of his teammates dragged him away to keep him from being stepped on. Not much later, a second opponent was dismantled by Manco and a bulky teammate working in series; Manco hit him high, the other hit him low, and he was carted away.

Seeing that inspired me to return to action, making it thirteen to thirteen. I was a little on the woozy side, but I functioned.

My return was well timed. The action was at the far end of the field, and I walked shakily toward it, filling my lungs with air, when abruptly someone delivered a tremendous kick and the ball came flying up the court toward me. I stared blankly at it a moment, watching the other players galloping in my direction and expecting to be ploughed under once again. They were almost upon me.

I had to do something.

So I began to dribble the ball, bouncing it off my forehead as rapidly as I could. As before, the mere act startled the opposing team into inactivity. They had never seen anyone do anything like that before. I glided through their ranks, heading toward the goal.

The squat, big-muscled Aztec who was the captain of the other team finally came after me. I stayed a hop and a skip ahead of him. Our men were cleverly forming a barrier around our goal. Manco Huascar stood to one side of the goal, Topiltzin to the other, and four or five teammates were lined up in front of them to protect them.

I gave the ball a looping kick and it soared over a dozen heads, passing into the circle of protectors and landing almost at Topiltzin's feet. Topiltzin scooped it up with his left armshield and tossed it to Manco Huascar, who poked it with his knee and sent it soaring toward the goal.

He missed by inches. As the ball trickled off on the other side, I felt a terrific blow between my shoulder-blades and toppled forward. The squat Aztec had caught up with me at last. But he was too late, for I had already passed the ball. I rolled over, pulling chunks of dirt from my face, and looked up.

And saw Topiltzin win the game.

The rebound from Manco Huascar's shot had

landed right where the Aztec prince was standing. He tapped the ball with his elbow, and it slid lazily upward, seemingly doomed to fall short, caught on the rim of the goal, teetered there for a thousand years, and dropped through. The spectators let out a deafening roar. The losing team dropped to the ground en masse in limp dejection. The winning team capered in wild delight. I dragged myself from the ground and rushed toward the prince, shouting, "Great shot, Topiltzin! Great shot!"

He swung from the heels and laid me full length on the ground with an unexpected punch in the jaw.

I got up with the taste of blood in my mouth and was ready to go for him then and there. But suddenly Manco Huascar was at my side, and the Inca whispered in that feathery voice of his, "You fool, you called him by his rightful name! Do you want him imprisoned?"

My cheeks flushed with shame. But in the uproar of the crowd, no one seemed to have heard. The celebration of victory went on and on. Topiltzin had walked over to the mound of wagered treasure. The rest of us followed. I hardly dared look the prince in the eye.

But Topiltzin seemed to bear no malice for my moment of stupidity, having discharged his annoyance with that explosive blow. He turned to me and said, "You, Englishman—without your strange style of play, we would not have won. Retrieve your belongings from the collection here, and then take your choice of the rest.''

Feeling honored and very conspicuous, I rummaged through the pile until I had found my ring and my knife. I touched the blade briefly to my lips to tell it how glad I was not to have lost it. Then I studied the heap and selected a splendid cape of feathers, red and blue and green, shimmering iridescently. It did not belong to any of my teammates, and so it was mine. I donned it proudly. Such a peacock cape I had dreamed of owning since a boy, and now it was mine!

Some further trophies fell to me in the later division of the spoils: two quills full of gold dust, a lustrous jade armlet, and a set of mother-of-pearl earplugs. Since my ears were not pierced, I traded them to another player for an intricately worked bone ring. In my cape and ornaments, I was beginning to look very much the Aztec dandy; but the golden hair and fair skin spoiled the image.

We divested ourselves of our playing costume and left the stadium, returning by canoe to the dilapidated building where Topiltzin lived. Not until we were inside did he remove his mask.

"You played well, Dan Beauchamp," he told me. "You wear a man's bruises now."

"Too many of them," I said. "You Aztecs have strenuous pleasures."

"The game was a short one," said Manco Huascar. "We barely had warmed up."

Sagaman Musa chuckled. "I had the best time

of all. I cheered loudly. Without my encouragement you would not have won, perhaps.''

I glared at him. "Why are you exempt from playing?"

"It is against my religion to take part in such sport," said the deep-voiced African gravely.

"Yes," said Manco Huascar. "He's orthodox. An orthodox coward."

Instead of showing anger, the black man merely laughed. Another man, called a coward to his face, might have gone for his dagger. But I thought I understood the African's way of thinking, and later I saw I was right. Only a man who doubts his own bravery bristles when called a coward. Sagaman Musa knew his own strength and his own courage, and had no need to prove anything to anyone. He did not like to play the rough game; therefore, he did not play.

Topiltzin said to me, "Will you join us on our expedition, Dan?"

"You know I will!"

"Good. We can use your agility and your toughness. We are bound on a bold adventure, which if successful will make me a king and yourselves rich men."

Briefly he outlined the plan. To the north, on the other side of the great desert that occupies much of northern Mexico and the southwestern corner of the Upper Hesperides, lay a land of placid farming folk. They had twenty or thirty towns, with names like Zuni, Acoma, Taos, and Cochiti.

Despite the dryness of their country, their fields were fertile and they produced a surplus of food, as well as handsome pottery and elegant jewelry.

In theory, this group of towns was subject to Aztec rule. The Aztecs had established protectorates in most parts of the northern continent. The local inhabitants, usually rather simple people, paid tribute to the Aztecs out of their surplus produce, and in return, for what it was worth, the Aztecs protected them against possible invasion by some other country. Rumors frequently circulated that the Incas, having seized all of the Lower Hesperides long ago, were thinking of invading the north, or that the Russians, with their trading outposts on the western coast, toyed with the idea of acquiring some inland territory. Topiltzin told me that many of these rumors were started by the Aztecs themselves, simply to cement their grip on the people of the Upper Hesperides.

The Aztec grip on the farmers of the southwest was rather weak at the moment, said Topiltzin. It was three hundred years since there had last been a revolt against the Aztecs in that region, and as a result Mexican rule was taken for granted there. A skeleton force stationed at the village of Taos was the only Aztec garrison in the entire district—fifty men, according to Topiltzin.

His plan was to attack that garrison. Taking it by surprise, he would execute all men who refused to swear allegiance to him. Then he would proclaim himself king of that part of the world. All tribute thereafter would be paid to him—and divided among his loyal followers. The tireless farmers would work for our benefit, and I would be an earl in the land of the mud houses.

"But that's treason!" I exclaimed. "You can't just steal a province of the empire! Your uncle Moctezuma would send an army to punish you instantly!"

"I doubt it," Topiltzin drawled lazily. "I happen to know that the King is planning military action in another zone entirely." He threw a sidelong glance at Manco Huascar. "The war with the Incas, long talked of, may soon be a reality. He will not want to divert troops to the north. Besides, I suspect that he would be willing to let me have my little kingdom. Its loss would be no blow to Mexico, and he'd be rid of my presence at court. We can't fail. Of course, if you don't want to go along—"

"I'll go," I said hastily. There was no future for me in Mexico, and this kind of empire-building expedition was more or less what I had hoped to become involved in.

"Fine. Everything is ready. We leave tomorrow, Seven Eagle."

I gulped. "But—"

"But what?"

"I'm due to be presented at court tomorrow! Quequex is taking me to the King!"

"There is no time to wait. For months now we

have worked toward setting out on Seven Eagle. I cannot postpone it.''

For one uncomfortable moment I wrestled between seeing the royal court and setting out with Topiltzin. Then ambition prevailed over curiosity, and I abandoned my hope of visiting the splendor of the palace.

''I'll visit the King some other time,'' I said. ''I'm going with you!''

EIGHT

We Overestimate Ourselves

I DINED with Topiltzin that night, and dined well, but I slept in my hotel room. In between dining and sleeping I went to search for Quequex, for I could not leave Tenochtitlan without seeing him again.

In a city of nine million souls, how do you find one fleshy charlatan if you don't know where he lives? I had surprisingly little difficulty. Since he was a sorcerer by profession, I sniffed around the religious quarter first, going to the Great Pyramid and hunting out a priest. I asked for Quequex and was told, "He is with the King." So I crossed the Plaza to the palace. I could not enter, of course, but I gave a slave my message, and after a while he returned to say, "Quequex will see you."

I was conducted to an inner room in one of the minor buildings of the palace complex. Quequex rose when I entered, his chins atremble, and touched his hand to my forehead in some sort of benediction. He looked solemn, but his eyes were twinkling.

Before I could speak he said, "You played well today."

"You saw me?"

"Everyone saw you. There is much talk of you, Dan. The King himself is eager to know you. You'll make your fortune here yet, boy."

I looked shamefacedly at the mosaic floor and said in a little voice, "I won't be seeing the King tomorrow."

"That devil Topiltzin! He's led you astray!"

"How—?"

"He was in the game today, wasn't he? The tall one, the one who scored the goal. Come, you can tell me. I spread no tales. That was Topiltzin!"

"Yes," I admitted miserably.

"So you saw him, against my advice. You let yourself be swayed by him. And now, instead of accepting the honor of a royal audience tomorrow, you will go off on his foolish adventure and die in the desert."

"You know of that?"

"Of course I know of that," said Quequex. "It's my business to know of everything. Topiltzin has been organizing this madness for nearly a year. To invade the peaceful farmers, to make himself a king—of course. Of course. And you've been taken in by him. I thought you had more sense.''

"Quequex, I'm sorry. I didn't come to Mexico to touch hands with kings, really. I came to do the sort of thing I'll be doing with Topiltzin.''

His face drooped, and the animation went out of it. ''I know. You're young, and you're bold, and you're foolish, or you wouldn't have left home in the first place. And you won't listen to me. I have seen this all in your future.''

"You can see the future?''

"Of course!''

"Tell me, then, what lies ahead for me.''

"You would not want to know.''

"Tell me, Quequex! If you can see it, tell me!''

He sighed and led me over to a marble pedestal on which stood a polished sphere of jade of such a deep green hue that it was the color of the depths of the sea, and I looked into its shining core and saw worlds within worlds.

Quequex said, ''You recall what I told you of the Gate of Worlds? This sphere helps me see beyond the Gate. But one thing alone is uncertain: I do not know whether I see the real world, or some phantom world of another future line.''

"What do you see of our expedition?''

"Death and disaster.''

"What will happen to Topiltzin? Will he be a king?''

"He will have an early death.''

"And I?''

"Wanderings and sufferings. You will see many nations. You will fall among spies and villains. You will flee from the Hesperides."

"No."

"I tell you only what I see."

"It's some other future line, I know it is!"

"If you enjoy deluding yourself, go ahead," said Quequex. "You are at the splitting-point of two lines now. If you go with Topiltzin tomorrow, one chain of events will ensue. If you remain here and meet King Moctezuma, your line will be different. Stand at the Gate of Worlds, and you can see them all. But you yourself can travel only one path, and you choose that path tomorrow."

"What else do you see?" I prodded.

"Dark hair, dark eyes, a laughing face. An ocean voyage. Violence. A scar on your flesh. A deep longing for someone you have lost. Tears and laughter."

"Is this the real world you see?"

"I cannot say. Stay in Tenochtitlan a while longer," he urged.

"I must go with Topiltzin."

"For him, a speedy grave. For you, much hardship."

"I'll risk it," I said. "Thanks for all your help, Quequex. I'll never forget you. Perhaps we'll meet again."

He looked at the jade sphere.

"We will never meet again," he said sadly, softly, and pressed my hand between his. Then he smiled. "Perhaps you will be a rich man after all, Dan Beauchamp. But it may not happen soon."

I went out from there, a considerably sobered man. But as I passed through the outer gate of the palace complex it occurred to me that if Quequex could really see the future, he might well have picked a different hotel in Chalchiuhcueyecan and thus avoided that pair of bandits. Unless, of course, his second sight told him also that he would be rescued and come to no harm. My head throbbed with bewilderment. I went to my hotel and tried to sleep.

At daybreak Sagaman Musa thundered on the door of my room.

"Wake up! Wake up! We're leaving!"

I groped to the door. "So soon? We've hours yet!"

"Plans are changed. We leave early. Come with me."

I washed and dressed and gathered my belongings together. The African had a motorcar idling outside, its boiler hissing with steam. I paid my bill. We left. Shortly we were passing out of Tenochtitlan by the western causeway.

Mists of dawn still hovered on the hill of Chapultepec as Topiltzin's little army assembled. He had six motorcars, of varying ages and conditions, and about thirty men. The army was a mixed lot: mostly Aztecs, but a sprinkling of redskins from the eastern part of the Upper Hesperides, a

couple of Chibchas from the Inca province of
Bogota, and a fugitive medicine man from a fishing village on the northern continent's northwest
coast. And, of course, one Inca—Manco Huascar—
and one African—Sagaman Musa. And an Englishman named Beauchamp. The three of us were the
lieutenants, Topiltzin the general. I admitted I could
drive, and Topiltzin put me in one of the cars, in
command of the two Chibchas, the medicine man,
and a sleepy-looking Aztec named Tezozomoc.

Our boilers were lit. Topiltzin, in the lead car,
gave a signal. Our creaky, sputtering caravan surged
forward, northward bound to adventure and empire.

I'll skip lightly over the details of our journey.
A dreary trip it was, but why inflict that dreariness
on you? We drove through unending dry heat, and
I who was accustomed to autumn fog and chill did
not enjoy this desert climate. The Aztec road was
superb as far as it went, but it went only a hundred
fifty miles north of Tenochtitlan. After that, we
had a road of lesser quality for a while, which at
least was paved, and finally we found ourselves on
a simple dirt track studded with bits of gravel. If it
had rained, we would have been wallowing in a
sea of mud. But I don't think it has rained in that
region of Mexico since the twelfth century, at the
latest.

Dryness.

Dryness everywhere: the land burnt brown by
the sun, no grass, no trees, only stunted thorny
little graygreen shrubs sticking out of the sandy

ground. To our left, most of the way north, a range of mighty mountains paralleled our route. To the right all was desert. In the day the heat was unbearable; at night the temperature fell fast, and we shivered and cursed. We went days at a time without seeing other human beings; then we would come upon tribes of desert barbarians, and small company they were! From them we bought such provisions as they had to offer. But we would have perished nine times over had we not brought most of our own food and drink with us from Tenochtitlan.

The motorcars were unreliable, and at least one of them broke down every day—usually in the hottest hour. Repairs were a time-consuming business. Sagaman Musa was our chief mechanic; I learned that in Africa he once had owned a factory that made cars and steam engines; but, so Manco Huascar whispered, he had become involved in unwise speculations and was bankrupted. I sympathized, remembering my father's own unhappy finances. Like Sagaman Musa, he had tried to get too rich too fast, and had lost everything instead.

Stripped down to a breechcloth, the man from Mali spent lone hours underneath our cars, tinkering with them until the boiler would boil again and the engine turn. His coal-black skin could stand the devilish sun well enough; I kept covered, though, and I noticed that even the Mexicans avoided exposing themselves. It was nothing for Sagaman

Musa to go practically naked as he worked. Sweat gave his body a magnificent sheen. Now and then he would punctuate his work with an astonishing stream of unintelligible African profanity, mingled with African obscenity, all in that ultra-deep opera-singer voice of his. And then he would rise, flicking sand from his skin, and say, "I think we can continue now."

I learned to handle a pistol on the trip. Topiltzin had brought guns for all, and whenever the caravan halted for repairs, which was often, he decreed a session of target practice. I had never fired small-arms before, and mistrusted them mightily, for I had heard that the powder has a nasty way of exploding in the barrel and killing the one who shoots. But that never happened with these Mexican weapons. My first few shots kicked up tufts of sand short of the target; then I got the hang of it and blazed away merrily at the tall, gnarled leafless things called cactuses, which made a satisfying plonking sound when they were hit.

Then, too, we had knife-throwing practice, for when a man's powder is wet he can still use his knife. I was the tutor here. I showed them how to grip the knife, how to stand, how to aim, how to make the muscles of the back do their work, how to throw—*thwick!*—and land the blade deep within its objective. I didn't mind giving such lessons, for I was easily the best knife in our company, and what man takes offense at having others admiringly watch him perform?

In the chilly evenings we sat around fires of dry desert wood and talked. I got to know my three fellow officers fairly well, though I had little to do with our common soldiers.

Topiltzin: ambitious and lazy all at once, keenly intelligent, a lively companion, very much skeptical of Aztec greatness and not at all awed by what his people had done. He had a streak of arrogance in him as broad as the Ocean Sea, but perhaps that was forgivable, he being the nephew of one of the world's greatest kings. Now and then Topiltzin treated us somewhat like servants, but it was apparently unintentional. I liked him, once I got past his surface mannerisms, the drawl, the aloofness.

Sagaman Musa: a shrewd, deep man, older than the rest of us, physically powerful, self-confident, self-contained. He talked a great deal, but said very little about himself. I knew he had come to Mexico for much the same reasons as I—to recoup lost fortunes and win power. He told many jokes, few of them fit for polite company, and talked much of world politics. I didn't mind his endless talking, because his rich, melodious voice fell easily on the ears, and when I got tired of what he was saying I merely tuned out the sense and listened to the sound as pure sound.

Manco Huascar: a mystery. He claimed to be, like Topiltzin, of royal blood. Yet Topiltzin conducted himself always as a monarch might, while Manco Huascar put on no regal airs. He never told us just how closely he was related to the Inca, or

Emperor, of Peru, nor did he reveal what he had done to earn himself exile. In fact, he told us very little of anything, and did far more listening than talking. He was a pleasant enough companion, but gave nothing of himself.

We talked of what we would do when we were rulers. "Build a palace for myself," said Topiltzin, "with a hunting park of vast size." Said Sagaman Musa, "Gather my money until I can bathe in it, and then return to Mali and buy a lordly estate." And Manco Huascar: "To take a hundred wives and found an Inca dynasty in the northlands." Lastly, Dan Beauchamp, who said piously, "I will send money to my family in England, and make them rich beyond their dreams. And then I will travel around the world."

"Go to Africa first," said Sagaman Musa. "Africa is the coming land of glory. The Aztecs have had their day. The Incas are finished. The Russians, the Turks—on their way out. You will see the future arise in Mali, in Ghana, in Songhay, in the black kingdoms. It is our turn now."

Topiltzin and Manco Huascar both looked irritated at Sagaman Musa's casual dismissal of the Aztecs and Incas, but they said nothing. I spoke up: "Does anything in Africa match the splendor of Tenochtitlan?"

"Give us fifty years! We are just beginning!"

"Why have you waited so long?" asked Topiltzin. "Man was created in Africa no later than he was in Mexico or Peru."

"China was great long before Mexico. Egypt was great before China. The scepter of greatness moves from land to land. Only now is it reaching us," said Sagaman Musa.

"Then what are you doing here?" goaded Manco Huascar. "Why not stay home and wait for the scepter to arrive?"

It was the African's turn to look irritated. "I am here because I am here," he said stonily. "But listen to my words; we will live to see Peru and Mexico rot as the Turks have rotted."

"Impossible!" blazed Topiltzin. "Our empire—"

"The Turkish empire," said Sagaman Musa, "once stretched frsm Baghdad in the east to London in the west. What do they have now? A few wretched countries centered on Istanbul! True, they've left their language and their religion behind in Europe—the ghost of an empire. But what good does that do?" He jabbed a forefinger at Topiltzin's jade-decked chest. "The same will come to you, Aztec! Only be patient!"

Topiltzin sighed. "I have an odd feeling, Sagaman Musa, that you may be right."

The desert was still with us, now, but we had entered into our future empire. We had come to the land of farming villages.

Here through this world of dryness ran a river from north to south, and along the river there were villages and farms. The people belonged to that redskinned race that inhabits both the Hesperides, but they were as different from the Aztecs as the Aztecs were from the Incas. These were short, rather stocky people, tending a bit toward fatness, with round faces, full cheeks, snub noses. Their villages consisted of square huts of mud, roofed with wooden beams; in some places the houses were four or five stories high, veritable apartment houses, and in others they were only one or two stories high, arranged in long rows separated by streets. The color of the houses was the color of the local mud: pink or even vermilion to the south, and varying shades of brown, gray, or tan as we proceeded northward.

It was a dusty country. The late-year winds came down like knives, scraping away the sandy topsoil and strewing it in the air. Swirling dust-devils of brown or gray or tan sand cavorted in the streets and alleys of the town, whipped across the big plazas, danced into the barely-open windows of our cars. I have never seen so much dust in my life, nor have I ever eaten so much, for the flat cornmeal cakes we were given tasted gritty with sand. (Topiltzin explained that the sand was rubbed off the soft sandstone slabs on which the native women grind their cornmeal, but I maintain that the stuff blew into the meal from the streets.)

We had a friendly reception; the locals are hospitable people by nature, and in this case they could clearly recognize a lanky Aztec prince at the head of our force. Of course, they had no way of knowing that Topiltzin was a rebel prince on his way to overthrow the Taos garrison. No doubt they thought he was bringing reinforcements or replacements for the garrison. So we were treated well in each village up the string. We stayed to the east side of the river, where the mud towns had names like Isleta, Sandia, Tesuque, Nambe, Picuris. There were just as many on the other side, but this was a mission of war, not a tourist trip, so we did not visit them.

We camped at Picuris—a handsome place in a cool valley flanked by pine-covered mountains—to plot the strategy of our attack.

If you're inclined to moralizing, you're probably telling yourself that a nice English boy like me had no business on this campaign of conquest. Wrong. Because we weren't making war against the farming folk; we were simply attacking a garrison of Aztecs.

I wouldn't have gone along with any attack on the farmers. I'm no Turk, and I won't impose rule by force. But the farmers have already accepted Aztec "protection," more or less voluntarily, and all we proposed to do was substitute on bunch of protectors for another. If anything, we'd be kinder masters than the present set. Incidentally, we'd get rich on the tribute we received, but that wasn't immoral or unethical, since we planned to give value for value by protecting the locals. There was plenty to protect them from, not only mythical Inca invasions but also the very real attacks by nomad marauders living to the north in the desert and on the great plains. The nomads had stolen horses from civilized folk, and now were breeding them and launching troublesome raids.

At our planning session, Sagaman Musa suggested that we inform the local people who we were and why we had come, and get their help in defeating the garrison. Presumably they'd be glad to rebel against the Taos soldiers.

"No," said Topiltzin. He said it in a way that left no doubt it was a final no.

"Why?" asked Sagaman Musa.

Topiltzin ticked the reasons off on his fingers. "One, because these people are poor fighters. Two, because they may not want to help us anyway. Three, because I have no spare weapons to give them, and they have none themselves. And four, because we're able to do the job without help."

There you have it: the stubborn pride of an Aztec. *We're able to do the job without help.* Translation: *It wouldn't be manly to let these peasants help us.*

Manliness! Even though he pretended to be different from the run-of-the-mill Aztec imperialist, Topiltzin at heart was like the others, worried constantly about proving his manhood. An Aztec went into the ball court and got his brains beaten our for days on end to show how tough he was. An Aztec danced barefoot in the sun on hot rocks. An Aztec whipped himself with thorny cords at religious festivals. An Aztec fought like a demon, deliberately outnumbering himself, to show what a hero he was.

We had the first authentic quarrel of our expedition. There had been plenty of bickering and jollying as the Aztec and the Inca and the African teased each other, but that had been for fun. Sagaman Musa was furious, now. As I've noted before, he was much calmer about this manhood thing than any Aztec would be, and he felt he had nothing to prove. He was here to win a battle by any means, not to show his courage in the face of great odds. He saw thousands of potential allies in these villages. He saw the defeat of the garrison without the firing of a shot, for how could fifty men fight back when surrounded by thousands.

He paced up and down, kicking angrily at the ground, pounding his massive fists into his thighs, shouting at Topiltzin, frothing in rage. A vein bulbed ominously on his broad, glossy forehead.

Topiltzin listened. He looked outwardly calm, but I could tell he was angry beneath. When Sagaman Musa finished exploding, Topiltzin said quietly, "We will not use these people as our allies. Those who lack the courage to carry out the attack as originally planned may return to Tenoch-titlan. We will prevail here, even if there are but ten of us."

Sagaman Musa let the air out of his nostrils in a long harsh snort. I wouldn't have been surprised to see flames come shooting out, too, he was that angry. Hostile words came boiling up in him. I believe he came close to saying things that would have destroyed any hope of co-operation between him and Topiltzin.

But with a visible effort he shut his lips down on the words before they could escape. He gulped and closed his eyes. Then he said, "Is this the last word, Topiltzin?"

"It is. Will you go back to Tenochtitlan?"

"I will stay."

And so he did, though he didn't try to hide his disapproval of Topiltzin's plan.

Which was:

To sneak up on the Taos garrison at night, overpower the guards, and thrust burning torches through the windows. The straw mats on the floor would ignite and the garrison would be smoked out. As they left the building, we'd pick them off one by one. Simple? Yes. Safe? Obviously.

From a common-sense point of view, Sagaman Musa's ideas had merit. In warfare, you always want all the extra troops you can get. But I confess I was glad Topiltzin had overruled him. This was my first battle, remember, and at the age of eighteen-years-plus-three-months I had a bit of manhood-proving to do myself. I wanted to fight. I wanted to draw some blood. I wanted to take part in a glorious triumph over extreme odds. Call me a fool and you'd be right, but that's how it was.

At dawn we began to march toward Taos.

It was a distance of some thirty or forty miles from our camp, I believe. We borrowed horses from the Picuris people, because these roads were unfit for motorcars, and in any event motorcars can be heard miles away in this quite land. Our pace was deliberately slow. At nightfall we camped ourselves a mile or so outside of Taos. We ate and rested. The plan was to attack in the small hours of the night.

At midnight we readied our torches and loaded our guns. Three hours later, we marched on foot into the village of Taos. Taos consists of two imposing apartment houses of tawny mud, five stories high, facing each other across a narrow brook. Some wooden planks serve as bridges to connect the two parts of the village. All in all, it's a marvelously picturesque place.

On the east side of the brook the Aztec garrison was housed in a smaller two-story building of about a dozen and a half rooms. We filed toward it. A guard was posted at the entrance to the village itself, but we took him out of the picture with no trouble. Several other guards were sitting in front of the garrison building. The villagers seemed to be asleep, and so were the men of the garrison.

We were supposed to creep out of the shadows and club down the guards in a hurry. Then, lighting our torches and throwing them in the garrison windows, we would merely wait for the enemy to rush forward in confusion.

It didn't work that way.

We were still a hundred yards from the garrison,

slithering through the darkness with our eyes fixed on the three drowsy guards in the middle of the town, when a voice sang out from the rooftops:

"What ho, enemies! Enemies! Awake, awake, enemies!"

And the garrison came to life.

Who would have thought that they'd post a sentry on top of one of the appartment houses? Not I, not you, certainly not Topiltzin. But he had been there, watching us all the while, and now that we were in the middle of the village he had given the alarm.

I recalled all of Quequex' gloomy predictions, in which I had placed little faith hitherto. Death and disaster for our expedition, an early grave for Topiltzin, wanderings and sufferings for me—

"Kill them!" Topiltzin screamed. "Kill them all!"

He lit his torch and hurled it toward the building. The next moment there were Aztec soldiers all around us, and we were in the battle of our lives.

Despite Topiltzin's optimism, there was no hope of victory. Twenty or thirty of the defenders had rushed out to deal with us, and as many more were perched at the windows of their fort, picking us off with rifles and pistols. The best we could hope for was a decent retreat.

But the way was blocked by a line of defenders.

We formed a tight knot in the middle of the open plaza. Topiltzin still howled for attack, but the rest of us opted for withdrawal, and after a moment of surveying the scene he agreed with us. We moved toward the exit, blazing away as we went.

I saw Sagaman Musa fire five shots and kill five men. The sixth shot went astray, and then he leaped forward like a wild one and used his pistol as a hammer, clubbing down a pair of Aztecs in desperate fury. He was in the clear, now, swiftly heading toward the narrow path leading out of Taos.

As I watched, a garrison man stepped out of nowhere and took aim at Sagaman Musa's broad back. I did not hesitate. Having little trust in my pistol for some reason, I reached across my hip for my knife, and it sped to my hand, and my arm went up, and the knife flew swiftly and buried itself deep in the Aztec's back with an odd thunking sound. It was just as though I had hit the wall target in our crowded cabin aboard the *Xochitl*.

But I had killed a man.

It calls for a moment's reflection when you separate a man's soul from his body for the first time. So I stood there like an ox, pondering the cosmic whys and wherefores of it all. I stood there just long enough for a member of the garrison to take dead aim at me and fire.

By rights, I ought to be dead, because anyone stupid enough to stop and meditate in the midst of battle deserves a quick burial. No doubt somewhere beyond the Gate of Worlds there are a lot of dead Dan Beauchamps. But in our particular universe the bullet traced a fiery line through the skin and muscles of my left arm, leaving a bloody streak eight inches long. That woke me up. I dropped to the ground and went for my pistol, and while my attacker tried to take aim I put a bullet through his skull. This time I did not meditate. The second kill is not like the first.

My arm was throbbing mercilessly, but I was lucky to be alive. The ground was covered with cropses, most of them belonging to men I had eaten dinner with and laughed with only a short time before. Keeping low, I scuttered across the ground and yanked my knife from the body of the man I had thrown it at. Then, with bullets swishing above my head, I raced toward the escape route. Sagaman Musa had already disappeared. I caught sight of Manco Huascar with a bloodstain on his white tunic; he smiled to me and beckoned, and I discovered that he had found another way out of the village. We ran toward it.

I killed two more men before we reached it.

Just as we got there, I turned and saw Topiltzin running toward safety, the flaming torch still in his hand, a pistol in the other. Three garrison soldiers came toward him. Topiltzin flung his torch into the face of one of them and dropped another with a well-aimed shot.

From my hiding place I took aim at the third. I squeezed the trigger. My gun clicked.

No ammunition!

And as I watched in horror, the third man put a

bullet through the Aztec prince. Topiltzin toppled headlong, twitched a moment, and lay still.

"He's shot!" I whispered hoarsely to Manco Huascar. "We've got to get him!"

"Don't be a fool. He's dead. Save yourself!"

He ran off through the night. After a moment of hesitation, I followed him, leaving the sound and the fury of the battle far behind.

I thought of Quequex' prophecies: a scar for me, death for Topiltzin. Blood flowed down my arm, searing hot, and I knew I'd carry the mark of that bullet to my last day. As for Topiltzin, I had seen him die. I shivered at the thought that Quequex truly was a sorcerer.

Heart pounding, arm ablaze, mind cold with shock and dismay, I fled like a frightened rabbit until I no longer heard gunfire behind me.

NINE

To the Western Sea

AND that was how I failed to win an earldom in the southwestern Upper Hesperides. The expedition had been a total fiasco, an utter disaster.

The scattered survivors of Topiltzin's little army came together in the wilderness outside the village like scattered logs tossed on a whirlpool. There were about a dozen of us: one of the Chibchas, the fat Aztec Tezozomoc, the medicine man from the far northwest, and several others, incluidng Manco Huascar. At first we said nothing to one another. What can one say, in the moment after crushing defeat? We huddled in the underbrush, breathing hard, letting our thundering hearts subside a bit.

Most of us bore wounds. The medicine man, Klagatch, ministered to us. He spoke Nahuatl poorly, but he understood where we hurt, and he dealt with our pains. For me he cleansed the wound, covered it with dry grass, and bound it with thongs. The gods would have to do the rest. It was an ugly wound but not a deep one; the bullet had passed through my flesh without remaining, cutting a red track in the meat. It would heal in a while, and until it did I would be in pain, probably with some fever, and there was no help for that.

He took care of Manco Huascar, who had been shot in an odd place, through the thick muscle of the arm within the armpit, on the left side. Two inches to the right and the ball would have blown open his chest; as it was, it had passed through, leaving a clean little hole in the muscle. The Inca would suffer a while too.

Klagatch dressed the rest of us, and only then did he tend to his own wound, a nasty gash along his scalp. He said little as he worked. He was a light-skinned man, short and stocky, with a deep chest and powerful shoulders and a broad black mustache. His thick hair had a coppery-red tinge in the proper light, and his voice was deep, although not so deep as Sagaman Musa's. All these people of the Upper Hesperides have their own typical appearance. In England we thought of them all as redskins, simple savages roaming the vast woodlands and prairies of their sparsely populated continent, but I could see clearly how different Klagatch was from the natives of the mud villages here, or from Opothle and his men from the southeast.

We did not have the strength to move. Our horses were tethered nearby, but we were afraid to go to them, for fear the men of the garrison had discovered them and were waiting in ambush for us there. Don't mark it down as cowardice; I had had enough fighting and enough killing for one night. My wounded arm was starting to swell, anyway, and beads of sweat were glistening on my skin.

I was worried about Sagaman Musa. He had looked healthy enough when I had seen him escaping from Taos, but I had not seen him since, nor had any of the others who had come stumbling into our improvised camp. Had he been slain in the darkness? Or was he wandering alone somewhere out there? To search for him was out of the question, of course.

Crouching in the shrubbery, we planned our revised future.

Returning to Tenochtitlan did not seem advisable. With Topiltzin presumably dead, I had no reason to go back there, and it was the same for many of the others. The Mexicans among us were welcome to try a homeward trek, but I did not yearn to cross that desert again.

Especially without the motorcars. We had left them at Picuris, many miles to the south, and we did not dare go back to get them. Before we could arrive, the garrison would have sent word of the rebellion to other villages, and the natives would be hostile. Even though the electrical voice-transmitting machine is not yet perfected, news travels quickly in outposts like this. So the motor-cars had to be abandoned, along with whatever belongings we did not have with us. I felt a pang of sorrow at parting with my feather cape, which I had won so strenuously, and with Quequex' jade necklace, and with the rest of the money Nezahual-pilli had given me, and with the few possessions I had brought with me from home. But Mexican money would do me little good where I was heading, and it was not worth risking my freedom or my life to get back stone trinkets or feather garments.

Where I was heading was diagonally north across the continent, toward Klagatch's home by the shores of the Western Sea. He had come to Mexico five years ago as a slave, and had served as doctor to one of the royal princes until Topiltzin persuaded him to join the invasion. Klagatch's only thought in leaving Mexico was that he might someday get home. Now, with Topiltzin dead and any bond of loyalty dissolved, he was striking out for the north country. I was going with him. So was Manco Huascar. The others decided to go back to Mexico, and I did not stop them from trying.

In the grayness of the dawn Klagatch drew a rough map for us of the Upper Hesperides, and showed us where we were, and where we had to go. If you have the map in your mind, you know how the continent is shaped, roughly five-pointed, a squarish shape with a big projection attached in the south—Mexico—and another projection in the far northwest. Our destination now was a point just about halfway up the western coast, where there is a large island parallel to the shore for many miles to form an island sound.

According to Klagatch we had some mean desert country to cross first, but then the land would be cooler and more fertile. If we went on foot the trip would probably take us till next spring, five or six months. If we could obtain horses, we would reach his village in two months or less.

I had just made up my mind to go with Klagatch when we heard noise in the woods nearby—someone approaching. Manco Huascar pulled his pistol, and I clasped my knife. An instant later a bulky figure holding a gun stepped into our circle. We were so tense that we nearly jumped him before we realized he was Sagaman Musa.

"I thought it was you! I heard you miles away!" he rumbled. He laughed and tossed his gun to the ground. He had emptied it, I remembered, in the battle.

We greeted him happily. I told him of what had happened after his escape, of Topiltzin's death and the rout of the others. He nodded. He had expected defeat all along. He himself was unwounded. He did not seem aware that I had saved his life at Taos, and I did not tell him, of course.

He had his own idea of where he was heading next.

He said he was going due west to the sea, and he indicated it on Klagatch's map. He pointed to the place on the western coast where the land begins to curve eastward. Here, said Sagaman Musa, was a warm and lovely land where winter never comes, where the days are neither too hot nor too cold, and where at present neither the Aztecs nor the Russians, the two imperialist powers of the Upper Hesperides, had made any inroads. Sagaman Musa was planning to proclaim himself king there. He was willing to accept a few dukes. Were we interested?

Not Klagatch. He was going home.

Not Manco Huascar, either. Speaking up firmly, he said, "I'm sorry, friend. I go to the north with Klagatch."

That took me by surprise. I had expected the Inca to say he'd join Sagaman Musa, and then I would have done the same. Why did Manco Huascar opt for the Russian-infested north when he could have chosen the fertile west? I couldn't answer that. But it had never been easy to understand Manco Huascar's motives in anything. The Peruvian kept his eyes open and his mouth shut.

Sagaman Musa looked at me. "Well? Do I have a fair-haired companion as I go?"

I was torn in many ways. I wanted to go with the African, for a curious bond of affection had grown up between us since our first violent meeting, and I knew him for a brave and resourceful man. Then, too, there was that golden promise of an empire to win in the west.

But that empire might prove a phantom, as the one envisioned by Topiltzin had been. We might neither of us reach the western shore alive. I did not know the route, and neither did Sagaman Musa; the best we could do was point our noses toward the sunset and hope.

Whereas if I chose to go north to Klagatch's country, I'd have two companions, one of them a doctor, and in Klagatch I'd have a guide who knew the way and could speak the languages of the tribes we'd meet. I could get established up there somehow, and then perhaps go fortune-hunting elsewhere, when I had some money and some further experience.

I weighed my options and I said, "I'm sticking to my original plan, Sagaman Musa. Why don't you come with us?"

"I cannot. I have my own destiny to follow."

And so I said goodbye to him. He clasped my tanned hand in his great black fist and squeezed it until my fingers writhed in pain. Then I did the same to him, but he merely smiled as I did my worst.

It was starting to seem as though this adventure was nothing but a series of partings. Nezahualpilli—Quequex—Topiltzin—Sagaman Musa—as soon as I made a friend, I was destined to lose him. Now I had none left but Klagatch, with whom I could exchange perhaps a hundred understandable words, and Manco Huascar, who was too sly and elusive to be called a friend.

The first month of our northward journey was the worst.

We went on foot through desert country where the days were waking dreams of blistering heat and the nights were chilling to the bone. Then we began to rise into plateau country, cooler and more attractive to the eye. But we were into December, now, and snow fell frequently. It was quite usual to wake and find a light dusting of flakes over everything.

We were beyond Aztec power here. The Aztecs are strong in much of the eastern part of the Upper Hesperides, beyond the great river called the Mississippi. But in the west their strength lies only in the region directly bordering on Mexico. Further inland, the country is too bleak and the population too sparse to make conquest worthwhile for them, and in the northwest the Russians, coming across from Siberia, have staked out their own sphere of influence.

Once we had ascended the plateau, we forfeited any chance of acquiring horses. There were no farming villages here. Among the farmers, we might buy or borrow or even steal three horses, but this was an uninhabited wilderness, occupied only by widely scattered bands of nomads. They had horses, but not for sale.

So we slogged on, step by step by step. On a good day we might walk as much as twenty miles. On an average day we did no better than eight or ten, for there were no roads, and it was work to slash a path. On some days we actually showed a net loss in mileage covered. Those were the days when we bravely chose a path down some agreeable canyon, only to find that it ended in an impassable wall and we had to retrace our route to the beginning and back up a way.

For food, we used our ingenuity. Klagatch, with his medicine man's skill at nature, showed us which fruits and nuts and roots were edible. Since the autumn was over, we had less of a selection than we might have had, but we fared well enough.

We hunted for our meat. Our guns were useless, since we had expended nearly all our ammunition at Taos, and when we set out our only weapon was my knife. Klagatch and Manco Huascar fired their last bullets on the day of our departure. I felt sure that I could kill game with a throw of my knife, but I did not dare take the risk: what if some wounded animal ran off and vanished, my knife embedded in his flesh? Instead I used the precious knife to make other weapons. We carved bows from saplings and made bowstrings from the hide of a deer we killed in a deadfall pit. Klagatch showed us how to back our bows with sinew to give them a greater force. I whittled arrows from thin straight branches, sharpening them to a deadly point and cutting a notch for nocking at the other end. And then, like simple barbarians, we ranged the forest in search of game.

It was discouraging at first. Our bows were weak, and often when we shot an arrow it would fall to the ground at our feet with a feeble twang. We missed our aim much of the time, even Klagatch, for he was no hunter. When we struck, we frequently did not kill, and lost both prey and arrow.

But we learned. I became a good shot, Manco Huascar a fair one, and we sped many an arrow to its target. Deer and elk and moose dropped before our shafts, and occasionally birds and squirrels. I felt an unmanly pity for the beasts we slew, for I fear I don't really have the killer instinct. I don't have the starving instinct either, though, and so I fired away.

Day by day we reverted to the savage state.

After the first month, we were savage enough to have mastered forest life. We made furry robes for ourselves from the animals we had killed, and moccasins to protect us from the snowy ground. We developed skill at sniffing out caves where we could spend particularly unpleasant winter nights; some of them still bore signs of native inhabitants. We made sacks and put our excess meat in them, and froze the meat in the snow for later use, since the game was growing hard to find. We survived. I would not want to go through those first four weeks again for any amount of gold, but after that it became fun.

We had no problems of direction. The sun was our guide, rising to our right and setting to our left, and we made our route btween those extremes.

I kept a calendar of notches in a stick. I started it a few days after we had set out, and I wasn't quite sure whether it was the fourth day or the fifth since Taos, so its accuracy was open to some doubt. However, by my calendar a certain snowy day was the 25th of December, and I announced to my companions that Christmas had arrived.

"The birthday of your god," said Manco Huascar. "Yes!"

It had been a rugged week, and I did not have the energy to explain to the Inca the special sense in which Jesus both is and is not our god. Nor did I care to tell him that Jesus is "one of our three gods," for that would lead to more complications. But I felt that a Christian should do something in celebration of Christmas, no matter where he was, and therefore I said to them, "On this day every Christian rejoices and shows his joy in feasting and in making gifts. I'd like to have a Christmas feast, and I'd like you to be my guests."

Manco Huascar, smiling broadly, agreed. So did Klagatch, though I am not sure he really understood much of what was taking place.

First came the gift-giving. We did not have much to give one another. I drew Nezahualpilli's golden ring inlaid with fine turquoises from my finger and offered it to Klagatch. Klagatch presented Manco Huascar with a copper plate, four inches in diameter and engraved with a strange and eerie design, that had hung about his throat for many years. In turn Manco Huascar gave me a silver bracelet that bore a pattern of tiny dancing figures.

"Merry Christmas!" I cried.

And they shouted back, "Merry Christmas! Merry Christmas!"

"In Peru at this month," said Manco Huascar solemnly, "it is also a festival season. It is the time of Capac Raymi, the 'magnificent festival.' At that time the boys of a certain age are welcomed into manhood, and sports and games are played, and the great golden chain is carried through the streets of our capital of Cuzco."

"Happy Capac Raymi," I said impulsively, and Klagatch echoed it, "Happy Capac Raymi!"

We defrosted a hunk of moose meat and built a fire. Selected nuts and roots from our collected supply were the garnishes for our feast. I spoke briefly of the significance of Christmas, choosing my Nahuatl words with care so Klagatch and Manco Huascar would understand. I told of the Three Wise Men, and of the manger, and of the star above, and of the shepherds in the field. I told of the Child and who He was and what He meant to those few of us in the world who were Christians. My two companions listened intently, though what their thoughts were I could not tell you.

Night fell on our Christmas feast, and I looked out from the cave over a snowy world illuminated by brilliant moonlight. It seemed to me that Christmas could not be complete without a Christmas carol. So I explained my wishes to them, and for half an hour I repeated the words, and then our voices rang out clearly in the crisp air, carrying a song of joy over the barren mountains and the bleak plains, bearing the glad tidings loudly enough for every Turk of Islam to hear the melody:

> *O Come, all ye faithful,*
> *Joyful and triumphant,*
> *Come ye, O come ye, to Bethlehem!*

And so was Christmas celebrated in the Upper Hesperides by one lonely Christian five thousand miles from home.

I thought much about home as I made that endless trek north. There was ample time for thinking, since neither of my companions was a talkative man, and hours of silence might go by without interruption. I thought of my father, that tall and thwarted man, and his flooded coal mine. I thought of my brother who had gone to serve in the army of the Turk, and how we had fought when I learned the bitter news. ("The Turks haven't been our enemies since the nineteenth century," he told me. "We won our war against them. We don't need to hate them now. These Turks aren't the same ones who conquered England way back then." But I punched him in the eye, all the same.) I thought of my sister in Moscow, or Moskva as she would probably say, and wondered if she really had loved that Russian enough to want to go to Russia with him. I even thought of my mother, and that was a rare thing, for she had died when I was very small.

Only four months had gone by since I had left home. It seemed like as many years. I had a scar, now, to show I was a man; the wound had closed, thanks to Klagatch, though I had had many a feverish night before the poison of infection left my veins. I had killed men. I had turned fat into muscle. I had known a sorcerer and I had known the nephew of a king. (I had chosen to put my faith in the wrong one of that pair, to my great sorrow.) And now I was bound for the end of the world on a crazy adventure without purpose. I will not lie in this work, for I am writing it mainly for myself, and a man who lies to himself is the worst liar of all. So I speak honestly when I say that the day did not pass on that march when I did not wish myself back in England. Huitzilopochtli himself could have come and plucked me from the ground and wafted me eastward over the Ocean Sea, and I would not have objected.

But of course there was no going home now. I could only continue on my present course, every step taking me further from England. I wished I had spent a moment in Mexico writing to my father to tell him I was well, for it would have been the proper thing to do. But things had happened swiftly when I was in Mexico, and I had not written, and now, of course, I was beyond any postal system's jurisdiction.

It seemed so long ago that I had sweltered in the foul heat of Chalchiuhcueyecan! So long since I had saved Quequex from those bandits! So long since I had played tlachtli in Tenochtitlan! Now the snow fell in mindless stubbornness. I had never seen such snow. In England we get some snow of a winter, but mainly fog. Here no fog, but an eternal cold whiteness against which neither boots of fur nor cloak of fur served as defense. The cold was more detestable than Mexico's lowland heat, I thought, although I recalled yearning for the bliss of an icy winter's day when I had been in the lowlands.

Late in January it began to look as though we would starve to death long before we saw Klagatch's village.

We had slain no game since shortly after the arrival of the New Year, and our supply of old meat was dwindling. Not even a squirrel made its appearance. So 1986 had been an unkind year thus far. It was snowing on and off much of the time, now, and often the weather was fantastically cold. By Klagatch's crude maps it seemed as though we had at least a thousand miles to go; though of course he had only an approximate idea of where we were.

Then came a violent day of many reversals in which our circumstances improved somewhat.

It began, in mid-morning, with the unexpected arrival of a lordly elk carrying a forest of antlers.

He was a proud beast, but we were hungry men, and as he loped over the snowy ground we brought him down with our bows. He writhed in a slow dying. I gave him the coup de grace with my knife, feeling pity and foodlust simultaneously. Then we began to skin him and dress the meat.

Taking apart some hundreds of pounds of freshly-killed elk is a complex task, and we were thoroughly absorbed in our work when the party of nomad readskins appeared. There were six of them, atop lean, scrawny horses, and they came down on us so suddenly that there was no hope of defense. One moment they were not there, the next they were. They were armed with crude rifles, spears, and bows.

I had heard terrible things of these wanderers of the wasteland. I fully expected to be murdered. But these men had no time to waste on murder.

They nudged their spears against our backs and marched us a short distance away. They went over us, looking for weapons. Our bows did not interest them, nor did they want my knife; they were after firearms. We had none, and they made no secret of their disappointment. They knocked us face-first into the snow. We could not fight back at spear-point.

There we lay, and it was worth our lives to look up. I breathed snow. I munched on snow. Snow crept within my fur robe. We could hear them grunting in their harsh language. And then, finally, we could hear them ride away.

Our elk was gone. Bloodstains in the snow alone remained.

Manco Huascar growled a terrible curse in his native language, Quechua. Klagatch kicked at the snow. I whisked the coldness out of my robe and stared balefully at the gray sky. We would starve to death, now. That was painfully evident. Food was scarce and it had been only luck that had brought us that elk, luck that would not be repeated. My stomach curdled at the thought of our loss. My imagination tormented me with counterfeit dreams of the rich taste of smouldering meat and streaming juices. But there was nothing to do but move on, and hope that our luck would change once again.

Bitterly dejected, we hiked another four miles that day. We were passing through forest country, now, where we could not see far ahead. There was little chance of finding an elk here. But we found a nomad camp instead.

Four men. Four horses.

Three of the nomads were busy over a fire, getting a meal ready. The fourth stood some twenty yards away from the others, watching the mounts.

We exchanged glances. We knew what we were going to do.

My knife was in my hand. Quietly we moved forward, until we were no more than a dozen feet away from the horses. They scented us, then, and a big, bony roan stallion reared up and whinnied.

The watchman turned around. In the same moment my knife soared through the gap between us and buried itself nearly hilt-deep in his chest. He fell without a sound. I wrenched the weapon free and leaped on the nearest horse, a sorrel mare. Manco Huascar was on the roan stallion. Klagatch was in the saddle of a third horse, and had his hand on the reins of the fourth.

I kicked at the mare's flank and off we went through the woods.

The three nomads were after us in a flash, of course. But men on foot are no match for men on horseback, and in the forest their arrows were of little use. Within five minutes we lost sight of them. We rode on for more than an hour, until we were far away in a sheltered box canyon, and there we halted for the night.

In the saddlebags of the stallion we found native food: dried meat, pounded with nuts and berries. I have had better fare, but just then I was not choosy.

You may say that we had done a wicked thing by killing a blameless stranger and stealing horses, leaving their masters marooned in a snowy waste. And I must reply that if you would survive in the wilderness, you must shape your morality to the circumstances. True, those four men had done us no harm, but their tribesmen had stolen our food and left us on the brink of famine. And no doubt our four victims would have done the same, if they had found us and not we them. This was not a country of saints. Thus we wasted little time in the niceties of the matter, but gripped our steeds and sped for the northwest.

Eight days later, with no food in sight, we killed the extra horse. I regretted that far more than I did the original theft of him. Fleshless-looking as he was, his meat lasted us a long time, while our remaining horses found fodder in unlikely-looking thorny shrubs jutting above the snow.

We were in monstrous solitude, now. We saw no other human beings, nor even their traces. There was less now here. Once there had been a vast volcanic eruption in these parts, it seemed, for the ground was black with ash over dozens of miles, and in one place we came to an outcropping of lava covering many acres. It was the most forlorn place in the world: a blotch of swirling ropy stuff, once molten and now cold as the tomb, that tinkled metallically when we tapped it. To Klagatch the lava zone seemed haunted. He prayed constantly as we passed through it, and at one point he shot a bird and spilled its blood in some ritual to propitiate the demon of the lava.

It was not necessary to slay any more horses. We entered pleasant country, relatively warm for winter, where it was rain and not snow that the heavens released. The trees were mighty, two hundred feet or more high and so bulky at the base that no European would easily believe it. There were villages at fair intervals where Klagatch could obtain food. The coast was near.

And at last came the moment when we reached

the Western Sea. It was a gray, stormy-looking ocean whose waves slapped against a dark-hued beach of eerie black sand. Klagatch pointed to the north.

"We are near my village," he said.

We rode through the shrubbery bordering the beach, and as if to celebrate the end of our journey the sun broke brightly through the clouds, and wearily we came to the shore village of Kuiu, our travels halted for at least a while.

TEN

TAKINAKTU

KUIU was no metropolis, but it would do. Considering the amount of open-air living I'd enjoyed all winter, I didn't require anything the size of Tenochtitlan.

We had arrived at a medium-big fishing village of about two thousand souls. It consisted of a lot of huge plank houses, more than a hundred feet long, in which whole families lived. Handsome canoes sixty feet in length were arranged in rows on the shore. Before each house stood a totem pole, carved in fanciful designs and painted in gaudy hues.

I do not understand what it is about these people of the Hesperides that leads them to see monsters. The Aztec gods, of course, are hideous things out of nightmare. Here at Kuiu the monsters had different shapes, but the effect was the same: an art based on horror. Each totem pole bore such an array of fangs and claws and beaks as I would like to see only when they are carved from wood. The canoes bore images of screaming faces. Even the blankets and clothing of these people burst forth in riotous color and a grotesquerie of images. The beaked and hook-nosed ritual masks that I saw in many homes added to the atmosphere of terror. These folk lived daily with demons. Yet they seemed prosperous and happy and far from savagery.

Since Klagatch had been gone nearly six years, his return aroused some awe. His wife, who had considered herself his widow, had remarried and now had two new children to go with the two she had by Klagatch. The whole family group came forward, including the extra husband, to greet the medicine man. No one seemed very disturbed over the situation, least of all Klagatch. Would the two men share the wife? Or would Klagatch take a new wife and everyone live happily ever after? I never found out, because I didn't stay long enough. The ceremonial purification of Klagatch—a welcoming-back ritual preliminary to any renewal of family relationships—was still going on when I took my leave of Kuiu.

We were taken in as guests by the Chief, Tlasotiwalis, who had the biggest house in the village. This barn-like structure must have been two hundred feet long. Inside it was divided into small dark cubicles, each holding a sub-family group of three or four people. Drying fish hung from the rafters, and fires blazed in earthen pits down the middle of the house. Since there were no windows, smoke collected quickly, and from time to time wall-slats were lifted to let some fresh air in. The roof was high, and the cooking fires provided the only light, so that the effect was one of constant flickering. I could see why these people were on such intimate terms with demons; simply to live in one of their houses was to see all kinds of shadowy shapes by the dancing firelight. The fact that the walls were hung with weird blankets, engraved copper plates, horrible masks, bearskin robes, and other such decorative objects added to the mood of horror.

I could not speak the language of these people, nor could any of them but Klagatch speak Nahuatl, and so there was not much in the way of communication between us. I smiled, and they smiled back, and that was about it. I learned nothing more than that they are people with fine teeth.

We were treated well. A huge feast was thrown for us on our first night, and the tables groaned under the weight of dozens of salmon. I ate more of this fish than I have ever eaten of any fish before; but it is a good one, with tasty red meat. Clams, berries, and mugs of fish oil accompanied the salmon. As we ate, shamans—medicine men— danced for us. They were scarcely human-looking, in their bearskin robes and their grotesque hook-

faced masks of red and green and yellow, and
some of them worked up a terrible frenzy. The
Kuiuans seemed to love every minute of it. The
more frightening the dance became, the more it
seemed as if the dancing shaman must soon fall
dead to the floor, the more the audience enjoyed
it. I saw Tlasotiwalis pounding the table with
delight.

Only one person in the room remained solemn
during the feast. That was Takinaktu, the Chief's
daughter. She sat beside Tlasotiwalis frozen-faced
and glum. If anything, she seemed a trifle revolted
by these noisy, barbaric carryings-on.

I confess I spent much of my evening studying
Takinaktu instead of watching the dancing. As I
remarked earlier in connection with my brief and
innocent encounter with the beautiful daughter of a
Mexican innkeeper, I have a tendency to fall in
love too easily. I see a pretty face and it instantly
becomes The Face, haunting my dreams, filling
me with absurd romantic notions. Luckily, I am
usually able to overcome these tendencies, which
is why I was still single, six months short of my
nineteenth birthday, in a world where early mar-
riages are the rule. I have been able to remind
myself that a lovely face is not the only requirement,
or even the most important requirement, for a
lifetime soul mate. And so I did not drop to my
knees to confess undying love to the innkeeper's
daughter, nor to a variety of nearly as attractive
girls I had known in England, nor even to Takinaktu.

But consider Takinaktu:

Seventeen years old, give or take a month. About five feet seven inches tall, perhaps a bit too tall for a man who is a quarter of an inch below six feet, but not seriously so. Fair skin, not coppery at all but rather somewhat Chinese in color and texture. Dark, straight, glossy hair. Alert, mischievous dark eyes. Prominent cheekbones, slender lips, firm chin, dimpled cheeks. A shapely and athletic-looking body.

Right then and there, sitting at the long table with the stink of salmon oil in my nostrils and the sting of smoky air in my eyes, I fell in love with her. She was across the table from me, not even looking in my direction, and so I could stare at her unabashedly. I let my mind roam imaginatively over a variety of possibilities. I saw myself introducing myself to Takinaktu, telling her of my travels and adventures, comparing her charms to those of Cleopatra and Helen of Troy, begging her to be mine. For the first time in my life I seriously could picture myself as a married man. I envisioned life with Takinaktu: the slim, laughing, dark-haired girl at my side, as strong as I was, able to swim far, run fast, climb mountains, bring down elk with a flick of her bow. I saw us carving out an empire somewhere in this sprawling continent, saw her ruling by my side in pomp and majesty.

Oh, a man my age can get wondrously foolish once he lets his mind ramble!

I brought myself back to earth with a jolt. Sternly I reminded my roaming imagination that I did not speak a word of Takinaktu's language, nor she any language I could speak. I told myself that she was an ignorant savage, unable to read and write, probably reeking permanently of fish oil, content with her little village and its hideous totem poles and masks. Quite likely she was already engaged to some muscular young man who was going to be the next chieftain of Kuiu. No doubt she and I did not have a single thing in common, for how could a London boy like me and a girl of the far west like Takinaktu possibly reach common ground?

Yet for all that she was beautiful, and she haunted my dreams that night as I tossed fitfully in my smokescented wooden cubicle within the great house.

In the morning I found myself alone. Klagatch was conferring with the shamans, and Manco Huascar had vanished I knew not where. Since there was no one else in the village I could speak to, I strolled down to the beach to have a look at the Western Sea.

For a long while I stared at its gray hugeness, thinking in wonderment that the fabled lands of Cathay and Japan lay out there somewhere. I was a long way from home. My heart beat a little more loudly than usual. Then I heard footsteps behind me.

Takinaktu appeared.

She was dressed in deerhide leggings, a poncho-like deerhide cape, and moccasins. She held a wickerwork cap loosely in one hand. Although last night at the feast she had looked sullen and bored, now she flashed at me such a brilliant smile that my kneecaps melted and I had to struggle to keep from sagging.

My cheeks flared hotly. Through my mind coursed all the silly thoughts I had had the night before about this girl. Now here I was, face to face with her, and I knew just how silly those thoughts had been. If she discovered miraculously what I was thinking, how she would laugh at my idiocy!

I smiled nervously and said in English, "Hello, Takinaktu."

"Was that English you were speaking?" she replied.

"That's right. And just about the first word of English I've spoken since—"

I stopped, trapped in a maze of linguistic confusion.

I had said hello in English. She had answered me in Turkish. I had answered her in Nahuatl.

Turkish? What was she doing speaking Turkish?

For an instant I thought this was a bad dream brought on by eating too much salmon. I said slowly and loudly in the Mexican tongue, "Do you speak Nahuatl?"

"No," she replied in Turkish, "but I can speak Turkish."

Now I think you realize I have certain patriotic prejudices against all things Turkish, including their language. However, like any sensible European, I *understand* Turkish; it's a necessary international language, little as I like to admit it. But to speak it is for me like fouling my mouth with rotten food.

It was either speak Turkish or hold no conversation with Takinaktu, though, and in that conflict you can guess which side won out. I shaped my tongue to the unaccustomed syllables and said, "I can hardly believe this. How did you ever learn Turkish, Takinaktu?"

"Russian merchants taught me. They brought me a book to study from, and now when they come here I speak Turkish with them."

"But why bother to learn it? What good is that language all the way out here?"

Takinaktu smiled that bone-melting smile again. "Because," she said in her soft, husky, infinitely wonderful voice, "because I wished to read Shakespeare in his original language."

You could have pickled up a dried salmon and hammered me four feet into the ground with it, and I would have been too bewildered to object. Here I was telling myself that this girl on the edge of the world is no more than an illiterate savage reeking of fish oil, and she stuns me twice by declaring that she's learned Europe's most important language so that she can read the works of England's greatest poet!

I stood there gaping for a moment.

"You are English?" she asked. "You have seen Stratford-on-Avon? You have lived by Westminster Abbey and the Thames? You have seen Shakespeare's plays produced?" The words left her in a rush.

In truth I am no student of literature, but what Englishman is there who has not been exposed to his dose of Shakespeare? I said, "Yes, of course, I've seen Shakespeare. I've seen *Julius Caesar* and *Macbeth* and *Suleiman the Magnificent*. And in school we read *Osman the Great* and *Hamlet*."

Takinaktu's eyes glowed. "Have you ever seen *The Fall of Constantinople?*"

"No," I said. And she began to quote from it.

I have to admit, Turkish or not, it is magnificent poetry. Shakespeare, like any Englishman of the sixteenth century, was required by law to use the language of the conquerors, but because he was Shakespeare he became a master of the tongue. His lines throbbed with life and vitality. They say that he hated writing plays about the Turkish sultans and their triumphs, that he would much rather have written of Richard III and King John and Henry IV, our Englisn kings before the Turkish Conquest. But he wrote of Turks in the Turkish tongue, and made such a job of it that to this day the Turks revere him and blush to think he was an Englishman.

Takinaktu went on and on, her voice rising and falling as she declaimed the lines. And she was good. She could almost have been a real actress. And then at last she stopped. There was a moment of awkward silence. Then she turned to me, her face afire, and said, "How wonderful to be in England! If you only knew how I wish I could get away from here!"

I should have seized her by the hands and cried, "Come, Takinaktu, fly with me!" Instead I mumbled something like, "I never thought I'd find a Shakespearean here."

She laughed. "Blame the Russians. If they hadn't come, I'd have been like the rest of my people. But they poisoned me with books. I hate it here. Skinning fish and giving feasts, carving those horrible masks—do you think I want to spend the rest of my life in this little village? I want to see the world, Dan! I've never been anywhere. I sit here reading my books and dreaming of escape."

"Why don't you escape, then?" I asked.

"I'm a chief's daughter. That makes me an important person. My father would send half the village after me."

"If you slipped away quietly, they'd never catch you."

"Perhaps," she said. "Perhaps. Or if I stowed away on a Russian trading ship. But I keep hesitating. I know what I should do, which way my destiny lies—but I don't follow it."

Her eyes looked deep into mine. Her face conveyed the intensity of her emotions. I can't begin to get down on paper the feelings I was experiencing. For here was a girl born six thousand miles from London who seemed as much a part of my soul as if we had once been one flesh. The same restlessness, the same eagerness to see what lies beyond the horizon—and yet in her an unwillingness to embark on the great adventure. I had known that same unwillingness, once, staring at the sea but fearing to set out on it, until that moment had come when I knew I must leave.

And so I trembled with inward excitement as I talked with Takinaktu. She was a living lesson in ignoring first impressions, for she was a sophisticated, keenly intelligent girl, better read than myself, bursting with ideas and dreams and hopes. She was not at all the greasy barbarian I had thought her to be. There was fierce energy in her, not yet harnessed. The thought of her sitting by this stormy sea shouting Shakespeare's immortal lines to the angry waves dazzled me.

We talked for more than an hour. She told me of her dreams, things she had never told anyone, told me how she longed to travel the world and sample its wonders, told me how she seethed with a terrible longing while she ticked off her years in this fishy village. And I told her of how I had been the same, and of how I had boarded the ship for Mexico, and of all the things that had befallen me since. During that hour I felt almost feverish with joy, and I think she felt the same way, for her face was flushed and her eyes blinked often.

We grew so close of soul, in fact, that it was as

if we had known each other from the cradle. And that frightened us so that we drew back. Takinaktu was the first to sense it and bring the talk to a less exalted level. Once she began to speak of commonplace things instead of deepest longings, I had no choice but to do the same, and so we dropped back from the conversation of intimates to the conversation of strangers. She told me things about local politics, about the weather, about the history of her village—blank, impersonal things. We could not, dared not, recapture the sudden fire of that earlier hour. And finally we left the beach and reentered the village.

I was in love, and this time it was the real thing beyond doubt. I was glad now that I had kept myself aloof from the daughters of innkeepers. I might have settled as a farmer in Shropshire last year, and never come to this forlorn western shore. And on that shore I had found the missing half of myself, if what the Greek sage says is true, that in mankind's dawn man and woman were joined in pairs, then cut asunder, and today the lonely halves seek out their missing companions.

In the village Takinaktu excused herself and entered a house, leaving me alone with my fantasies. I stood bemused a long while. Village boys came out and stared at me, eyes wide, I suppose because they had never seen a fair-haired man before. This is a continent of black hair, and the Russians who are the only outland visitors here are no fairer than the natives. I had let my beard grow since leaving

Tenochtitlan, so that in the pale March sunlight my head was a globe of gleaming gold, and that must have been what fascinated them so.

Manco Huascar came up to me while I was in this mood of airy rapture and clapped me on the back.

"Are you ill?" he asked.

"I? No. Why?"

"You look so strange!"

I wanted to blurt out to the Inca that I was in love. But I had never thought of Manco Huascar as a man with whom to share confidences; in all the months since he had introduced himself to me with his spear in Mexico, there had been no real closeness to him. We were traveling companions, not friends, and I did not know a thing about him, not his age nor why he had left Peru nor whether he had loved or married there nor what he was searching for in his roaming of the world. So I did not share my news of Takinaktu with him just then.

To cover my awkwardness I said, "Where have you been?"

"Speaking with Chief Tlasotiwalis. Come aside, where these children can't hear us. There's trouble afoot in this region, and perhaps we can profit from it."

We went back to the beach and leaned against an ornately carved canoe to talk. The Inca had sniffed out a great deal this morning, in the Chief's great house. It seemed that the natives were planning an uprising against the local Russian merchants.

The Russians first came to these parts about two hundred years ago. It was not a difficult journey for them, since they had long controlled the eastern half of Asia, and they simply sailed across from Siberia. At first their relationship with the coast people was a simple mercantile one; they exchanged nails, guns, cloth, beads, brass kettles, and the like for the furry skins of sea otter and beaver, much in demand elsewhere of coats and cloaks. The very hatchets with which these people carve their totem poles were brought to them by the Russians.

In time the visitors came to exert political control. They established trading posts along the coast that became powerful towns. Today they tell the native chiefs what to do, and the chiefs obey; the effect is to turn this entire area into a Russian colony. A rebellious tribe will be cut off from the supply of machined goods and weapons, forcing it to sink back into primitivism.

No one likes to be dependent on an alien master. The situation here had been going on for so long that both sides had come to take it for granted; but there were really only a few Russians and many natives here, and Chief Tlasotiwalis was chafing at the bit. "He wants to give the Russians an ultimatum," reported Manco Huascar. "Either they stop trying to dominate his people, or he'll drive them into the sea. He means it. He's a restless, impatient man with big ideas."

His daughter is much like him, then, I thought.

I said, "How does this friction benefit us?"

The Peruvian smiled. "We can go either way. We can warn the Russians what's afoot and ask for a rich reward. Or we can throw in our lot with Tlasotiwalis and help wipe the Russians out. Afterward, these people will need outside advisers. We'll be able to gain great influence here. We'll do what the Russians never thought of doing: welding all these scattered coastal towns into a strong nation."

"I don't like the idea of betraying these people to the Russians," I said.

"Neither do I," replied Manco Huascar quickly. "It was only a fleeting idea." But he wouldn't have put it forth in the first place unless he took it seriously, and I suspected he would have been perfectly willing to sell Tlasotiwalis out if I hadn't cooled the notion.

We hatched some plans. Then Manco Huascar took me in to see the Chief.

I felt embarrassed in his presence, inasmuch as I had spent most of the morning in passionate conversation with his daughter, learning from her how much she hated village life. But I forgot about Takinaktu quickly as I became enmeshed in the net of intrigue the burly chief was weaving.

In sign language coupled with a few expressive

grunts and some scattered Aztec words, Tlasotiwalis suggested that Manco Huascar and I go on a spying mission to the Russian enclave. We could insinuate ourselves within, pretending to be traveling diplomats, and make an accurate count of Russian strength, noting how many men they had, how many guns. After that, Tlasotiwalis would know the extent of his own relative power.

Once we were sure of what we were supposed to do, we signaled our agreement and the Chief called for some of the younger men of the village to take us to the Russian town. It was five or six miles to the north, up the coast. We went by canoe, a journey that took us most of the afternoon. Manco Huascar and I helped beach the canoe and approached the stockaded settlement. He whispered to me, "I am your servant. Otherwise they will wonder why I am with you."

A gate in the stockade opened and we were faced by a couple of well-armed fur-clad Russians. I bowed courteously to these minions of the Czar and said in English, "Good day, gentlemen. I'm Sir Daniel Beauchamp of His Majesty's Foreign Service, engaged in a transcontinental survey, and I'd like the pleasure of a visit."

"?" they said, in Russian.

As I had expected to do, I switched to Turkish, revenging myself on the language by speaking it in a thick Cockney accent. Once more I introduced myself. They looked uneasily at each other and muttered in Russian. Then one of them detached himself and went within the stockade.

He returned a few minutes later with a black-bearded Russian of middle years, huge of belly and creased of face, who was enveloped in a fur coat the size of a tent and wore hip-high leather boots. A strong odor of garlic emanated from him. His small eyes focused coldly on me and he floored me by saying *in English*, "I am Fyodr Ivanovitch Golubov, wishing to welcome you to our village. Sir Daniel, it is a pleasure. Your companion is whom?"

"My servant," I said glibly. "A Peruvian slave whom I purchased in Mexico. We are making a tour of the Upper Hesperides on behalf of His Majesty King Richard."

"Richard?" Golubov repeated, swishing the word around his mouth like a dentifrice. "Richard? But Edward IX is your king!"

"King Edward died Whitsuntide last," I said. "King Richard's coronation was held in the summer."

"A pity. Your king was a fine man. I served many years in your country. Diplomatic corps. Before transfer to this bleak place. We will have long talks of England, Sir Daniel, once you are my guest. But your credentials, please?"

I wanted to sink into the earth. Golubov a former diplomat stationed in London? Then he'd know all the protocols and formalities I was supposed to proffer. And I knew not a one. I stood there fumbling for words a moment before inspiration came, and then I said, "A thousand pardons, Fyodr Ivanovitch, but my papers along with most of my possessions were lost in a river accident on the Mississippi, which is why you see me in these rude clothes and in this unshaven state. But if you have your doubts, a letter to London will confirm my status—"

"—in only six months. But here you are today, asking admission. How do I know you are what you say you are? You may be a spy! And if I admitted you, and then it developed you were here falsely— ah, no. A thousand regrets, Sir Daniel, but I cannot to admit you."

It seemed pretty final. I was ready to give up and return to Kuiu with news of my rejection. Then inspiration struck again, and I thought of my Russian brother-in-law, who had once been on the Czarist Embassy Staff in London.

I said hastily, "Fyodr Ivanovitch, perhaps I can offer a character reference. Do you know Constantin Nikolaievich Kropotkin, formerly part of the Czar's diplomatic corps in London—that is, New Istanbul?"

He pondered. Heavy lids descended over the shiny little eyes. "A tall, thin man? Pointed beard? Great elegance of bearing? Fond of the ladies?"

"That's the one!"

"I remember him, yes. One of our younger

attachés. Formerly, you say? In New Istanbul no longer?"

"Recalled to Moscow several years ago. I knew him in diplomatic circles there. He is now the husband of my sister."

"Indeed?" said Fyodr Ivanovitch. He clapped me lustily on the shoulder. "Come in, then, Sir Daniel, come in! By all means!"

ELEVEN

TRAVELING ONCE MORE

GOLUBOV ushered us jovially into his village, and there began a night of feasting and revelry quite different from last night at Kuiu. There were no shamans here, no sinister masked figures—merely a few hundred Russian merchants with insatiable appetites. We gorged ourselves on mounds of smoked sturgeon and caviar, washing everything down with a cold, fiery Russian liquor clear as water but considerably more potent, and then came the bear-steaks, the pots of steaming vegetables, the bowls of hot soup.

The boys from Kuiu who had rowed us up here were left on the beach. I could not very well invite them in; and, in my guise as an English diplomat, I had to show callous disdain for the welfare of members of inferior races. So we ignored their plight, except that late in the evening I asked that some sturgeon and cold meat be sent out to them. It was done.

Golubov questioned me in detail about the purpose of my mission to the Hesperides, and I answered him as evasively as I could. He wanted to be brought up to date on the gossip of the diplomatic colony in London, too. Here I was at a disadvantage, but I did my best, leaning heavily on the names of people I had met through my brother-in-law, and retailing some of the tales he had told at our house while courting my sister. Golubov had not been in England for upwards of five years, which allowed me to point out that as a very junior member of the diplomatic corps I was in no position to have known most of the people he asked me about. He seemed to accept that.

When we had stuffed a sufficient quantity of food down, he took me on a tour of the stockaded village. I saw the storerooms where great piles of costly furs were awaiting the next ship to Russia. I saw the church, all decked with the ikons and symbols of the Russian Orthodox Church, a branch of Christianity about which I know very little. And I saw the armory. Golubov seemed to go out of his way to show me how well armed the village was. Rifles were stacked by the dozen, like cords of firewood. Boxes of ammunition, carefully protected against fire, reached to the ceiling. There were pistols, swords, explosive grenades, bayonets, cannons, smoke bombs—enough to stand off a major invasion.

I felt sorry for Chief Tlasotiwalis and his people. If anything was clear, it was that they were not going to throw off Russian oppression just yet. An attack on this village would mean suicide for the attackers. Golubov's kindness in showing me his armory made that indisputable.

After he had taken me around to display the village's strength, we returned to the main hall for another round of drinking and feasting. Then it was time for sleep, the Russians providing a comfortable room for us.

When we were alone for the first time that evening, Manco Huascar whispered, "There is no question what we do now, is there?"

"We don't lead any revolution, that's sure enough."

"No. Instead we sell our information to Golubov. He'll pay well for it."

"Betray the village?"

"I told you, we'd go to one side or the other. The fat Russian has much gold. We'll go to him in the morning and tell him what Kuiu is planning."

"We will not," I said.

"What's this? I thought we were partners in all deeds."

"Not this one. I won't sell Tlasotiwalis and his people for a few pieces of gold. And you won't either, Manco."

The Inca's face was furrowed with anger, but

his voice remained soft as he said, "Are you threatening me, Dan?"

"If that's what it sounds like, yes."

"How can you stop me?"

"It's very simple," I told him. "You're here as my servant. What I do is cry out that you've tried to kill me and steal my money. You'll be taken out and shot. The Russians would do that for me. You're only a slave to them, remember."

Manco Huascar was silent a long while. I could tell that my words had gone deep.

Then he said, "You would do this to me?"

"To save Kuiu, yes."

"What are those people to you? They're only savages!"

"One of them, Manco, reads Shakespeare. Do you read Shakespeare? Do you know who he is, perhaps? I like those people. One of them is Klagatch, remember, who bound our wounds and guided us halfway across this continent. Would you sell him to the Russians?"

"I don't mean to do them any harm," said the Inca gently. "I would only gain some profit by selling information. The Russians will not injure then unless they attack first, and when we return with news of these weapons here there will be no attack."

"Even so, it would make the Russians suspicious. They might stop trading with Kuiu. They might have Tlasotiwalis killed as a troublemaker. They might reduce the prices the village receives for its goods. Kuiu would suffer. It's not worth it in terms of what you'd receive. I'd kill you, Manco, if you did it.''

''I had not thought the village would suffer,'' he said.

He reconsidered, or pretended to reconsider, and promised me he would say nothing to Golubov about Tlasotiwalis' insurrectionist ideas. I knew he meant it, for while we were here I held the power of life or death over him, and that worried him. We patched over our quarrel and told one another that we still were friends. Yet that night I slept lightly, with my knife in my hand.

After a lavish breakfast we prepared to bid farewell to the Russian town. Fyodr Ivanovitch accompanied us to the gate, his fat hand resting heavily on my shoulder. He wished me well and asked me to carry his regards to several Russians in London. Then he said, ''Tell me truthly, now: is Constantin Nikolaievitch really your sister's husband?''

My cheeks blazed. ''Of course he is! Why?''

''If he is,'' said Golubov, ''then that is the only truthly thing you have told me since you came here, Sir Daniel. I believe that much, but no more. You are no member of His Majesty's Foreign Service. You are not even a good imitation. All the same, it has been of pleasure to know your company, and now I wish you a safe voyage onward.''

He pounded me amiably on the back and half-shoved me through the gate in the stockade. I felt humiliated as I walked down the beach toward our canoe. The old glutton! I hadn't fooled him for a moment!

The least he could have done, though, was let me believe I had taken him in.

"What was he saying, there at the end?" Manco Huascar asked.

"Nothing," I snapped glumly. "Just saying good-bye."

With Klagatch as our interpreter, we told Tlaso-tiwalis the nature of the enemy he had chosen to tackle. The Chief grew more and more somber as our lengthy recitation of guns and bullets and grenades went on, until at length he rose and stared into the fire on the earthen floor, kicking moodily at the embers around the pit. He said something in the local language to Klagatch. The medicine man told us that it was an expression of grief and frustration. Tlasotiwalis now realized that it was impossible overthrow the Russians.

"But he will attack them anyway," added Klagatch.

"No! You'll all be killed!"

The chief said something to Klagatch. He translated it: "There will be an attack by night. They will burn the stockade and kill the Russians while they sleep."

Manco Huascar and I knew a little about attacking armed garrisons by night. So did Klagatch, who had learned the same lesson with us at Taos.

I said to him, "Can't you tell the chief what happened when Topiltzin tried the same thing? It'll be a massacre!"

"I have told him. He will not listen. His mind is made up that the Russians must die."

There was no way to convince Tlasotiwalis of the impracticality of his idea. Not even if I had taken him up to Golubov's armory would he have wavered. Something in his soul compelled him to strike a blow for Kuiu's freedom, and I admired him for that, but I could not grow enthusiastic about a military campaign that was doomed before it began.

Outside the Chief's house, Manco Huascar said, "We will leave here tomorrow. I want no part of this war."

"Neither do I. But can't we stay a little longer?"

"If we do, the chief will expect us to help him in his fight. You saw the guns. It's best to leave before the trouble starts."

"Where will we go?"

"Peru," Manco Huascar said.

That stunned me. He was an exile, and had given me to understand that it would be worth his life for him to set foot in Cuzco again. Yet here he was blandly telling me he was going home, and inviting me to join him.

He saw the expression I wore, and quickly explained. He had gone abroad, he said, against the wishes of his followers, who wished him to lead a revolution against the Peruvian ruler, Inca

Capac Yupanqui V. For several years now he had been roaming the Hesperides, searching for some base of power from which he could ultimately launch an invasion of Peru. That was why he had affiliated himself with Topiltzin. But he had had no luck in this project, and so he had decided to take a direct approach: go back to Peru, rally his followers, and overthrow Capac Yupanqui. It could be done, he said, citing an episode of the sixteenth century when Inca Atahuallpa had dethroned his half-brother Huascar.

In retrospect, I know what I should have done. I should have ignored Manco Huascar's wild plans and headed south to find Sagaman Musa. I had made a serious mistake by parting with the African in order to stay with Manco in the first place. And my experience with attempted overthrows at Taos and here at Kuiu should have convinced me that if we could not conquer the garrison at Taos, we were not going to conquer Peru.

Yet it is easy to delude one's self with vain hopes. I had not yet shaken off the dream of empire. So I said yes to Manco Huascar, even though I was hardly eager to begin a new journey only two days after reaching the relative comfort of Kuiu. Nor did I feel a hurry to leave Takinaktu.

I went to her and told her something of what was happening.

"Your father will die in this war," I said. "Many men will die with him. Kuiu will be destroyed. Can't you do something to prevent him from this?"

"His mind is set on it. Nothing will sway him."

"I would have liked to stay here," I told her. "But not in a time of war. Kuiu will be full of widows next week this time. Manco and I are leaving tomorrow."

Her hand shot out and caught my wrist. "Take me with you!"

"What?"

"This is my chance to escape! In the confusion of the war, my father will never send men to search for me! Oh, take me, take me! Where are you going?"

"Peru."

Her eyes gleamed in wild excitement at the thought. I was less delighted, much as I wanted to keep Takinaktu with me. To travel thousands of miles with a girl—

She read my mind. "I can ride a horse," she said. "I can shoot a bow. And I can speak the languages of the tribes you'll meet. I'll be useful, I promise. You'll see: I'm as strong as you are. Wrestle with me. Here. Try to push me down."

She put the flat of her hand against the flat of my hand, and shoved. I saw what she was trying to do to get me off balance so that I'd have to lift a foot. I braced myself just in time, before she sent me stumbling.

Takinaktu had told the truth. Her wiry body was nearly as strong as mine. She could not push me over, now that I was braced, but for a long while neither could I defeat her. Then I felt her weakening.

I enjoyed the contact with her hand well enough not to want to win; at last, though, I showed my superiority and she yielded. We both laughed.

"Can I go with you?" she asked.

"Why not?" I said.

I told Manco Huascar. He was not pleased, but I told him that if Takinaktu did not go, I would remain here with her. The prospect of journeying thousands of miles alone must have seemed worse to him than traveling them with a seventeen-year-old girl, so he gave in.

We had to change our departure plans in order to provide for secrecy. Instead of leaving at morning, we would go in the depths of the night. The three horses on which Manco, Klagatch, and I had arrived were rested and well fed. Our few belongings were ready. We did not tell Tlasotiwalis that we were going. It was rascally repayment for his hospitality to slip away in the night like thieves, with or without his daughter, but we could not afford to have a formal farewell feast and risk any complications about our leaving.

In the darkest hour I rose and moved silently down the great house to the cubicle where Takinaktu slept. She was up and dressed when I arrived, and was putting some prized possessions into a leather bag. One of them was a thick, stubby little book bound in horsehide.

"What's that?" I whispered.

She showed it to me. Shakespeare, the complete works. In Turkish.

We left the building without incident. Manco Huascar was already at the horses. The moon was but a sliver that night, and if there were any night guards at the village, they were looking the other way.

Before we went to the horses, I took Takinaktu's hand and drew her close to me. Her eyes, meeting mine, were bright as polished obsidian. I said in a low voice, "One thing understood before we leave. There's no turning back, once we ride away. This is goodbye to Kuiu forever."

"Yes. Understood."

"Good. Come on, then."

We ran to the corral. Her long legs easily kept up with mine, and we arrived together. Manco Huascar had untethered the animals. I took the sorrel mare again, the Inca the roan stallion, and Takinaktu mounted the horse Klagatch had ridden. We looked uneasily at one another a moment. Then I nodded toward the southeast, and Manco Huascar slapped his mount's flank and left the corral. We followed.

Many hours later, a magnificent pink dawn exploded over the mountains that lay to the east of us. We had not looked back once. Takinaktu had proven the complete mistress of her horse, and I had no doubt that we'd reach our destination safely.

Something in me wanted to sing as that pale light filled the morning sky. True, I had won no kingdoms yet. But I was a free man, riding into open country with a strong horse beneath me and a beautiful girl at my side. I guess it was forgivable vanity to think of Takinaktu as "my" girl. In a way she was, although in some important ways she wasn't, as I found out later on.

Our route was clear. We would return to Mexico and take ship for Peru at Acapulco, the great seaport on Mexico's western coast. Because we were riding into springtime, we would suffer none of the hardships that we had known on our winter journey north from Taos to Kuiu. By late summer, we would be in Peru. I had no idea what part Takinaktu planned to play in our projected overthrow of the Peruvian government; perhaps that enterprise seemed as unreal and implausible to her as it did to me. But for the nonce we assumed we were actually going to do some such thing.

We traveled at an easy pace, covering many miles each day without strain. The weather was mild, and the plains that had been snow-covered in January now were bare and abounded in tender fodder for the horses. For our own food we brought down game from time to time—now a moose, now an elk, now a round furry bear. Takinaktu showed that she could handle a bow as well as either of us. She had no remorse about killing for food, either. I have always been fond of bears, and when we found our first one I stood a while philosophizing to myself over the propriety of shooting him, and while I did that Takinaktu nocked arrow after arrow and brought the beast down. You have not tasted steak until you've eaten steak of bear, either— blood-rare and juicy, and singed in the smoke of a crackling wood fire.

When we camped each night, Takinaktu and I had much to say to each other. Manco Huascar sat to one side, like the chaperone that he essentially was, looking sour about the whole thing. I was not much concerned with his feelings, though.

We talked of everything that came into our heads. At one point I told her about Quequex' notion of the Gate of Worlds. I conjured up a different world beyond the Gate in which the Turks had never mastered England and Shakespeare had been allowed to write in his native tongue. Then we played a game, trying to imagine the things he might have written.

That much was pleasant. But then Takinaktu's quick mind, which had seized instantly on that fanciful Gate concept, reached the final implications. "If Europe remained strong and healthy," she pointed out, "then by the sixteenth century population pressure would have driven some explorers west. And after the explorers would come the colonists. By now this whole continent would be a battleground for white men. Frenchmen, Spaniards, Englishmen, Russians—each coming in from a different corner, and meeting in the middle to struggle for supremacy. And the native people ground like corn between millstones."

"No," I said. "I doubt that that would happen."

But I said it weakly, for I knew she was right. Quequex had painted the same picture for me months before. Except for the lucky accident of a plague that had devastated Europe, we would have burst forth and conquered the world, for that was our nature before we were smitten. And any discussion of probable worlds quickly led to that same point: European colonies everywhere in the Hesperides, and the natives beneath our heels.

To console Takinaktu I offered a different maybe-world in which the Russians too had been wiped out by the Black Death, so that her people had had time to consolidate a strong empire of their own in their coastal strip. But she would have none of that one either.

"My people are not empire-builders," she said. "If the Russians had not come, we would have remained as you saw us: scattered villages in an uneasy truce. The difference is that with the Russians, we had metal tools. Without them, we would have been more primitive. And without them, Dan, I would never have read a line of Shakespeare."

I began to sense that I was running into trouble with this game, so we shifted our amusements somewhat. Takinaktu took out her much-thumbed volume of Shakespeare, and we read the plays out loud, she taking all the female parts, I all the male. It pained me to have to read Turkish, even such lovely Turkish as this, so I tried translating the lines into English, as poetically as possible. That was when I discovered that I was no poet.

Takinaktu, lying beside me in the moonlit dankness, begged me to go on speaking English. "I love the sound of it," she murmured. "It's so strange—those clicking, swooshing letters! Speak it again!"

I talked English to her until my throat went hoarse, but of course it was pure gibberish to her, just so much noise. I could do better than that. I started to teach her English.

We began our lessons beside a sparkling brook on a starry night, three weeks' journey south of Kuiu. Manco Huascar sat by himself, dangling a fishing pole into the water and yanking out one jiggling trout after another while I gave Takinaktu her first insight into the world's finest language.

I pointed to things and named them. That was the easiest part. "Tree," I said.

"Tree."

"Branch."

"Branch."

"Leaf."

"Leaf."

But then it grew harder. I couldn't simply point to the sky and say "sky," for how would she know I did not mean "stars," "clouds," "up," or many other things? So I had to fall back on Turkish equivalents. When we got to such things as verbs and adjectives, it was even tougher. But we persevered. The journey was long and there was little else to do.

Takinaktu learned quickly. In her part of the world, each native town speaks its own distinct dialect, amounting almost to a separate language, and it is necessary also to learn Russian. She had picked up Turkish besides. So she spoke many languages already, and someone who speaks five or six languages does not find it a chore to learn another one. It had been the same with me, to a lesser extent: knowing English, of course, and having reluctantly mastered Turkish as well, I had acquired the Mexican tongue with surprising ease.

Within a few days she could speak English, after a fashion. I fell into the habit of speaking to her in that language, and when possible she answered me. With Manco Huascar, of course, I went on speaking Nahuatl. He and Takinaktu spoke a dozen languages between them, but oddly there was no overlap at all, and they were unable to communicate with each other. If Manco Huascar and I had been better friends before, I might have gone out of my way to see to it that he was drawn into our company more. But I had never cared much for the Inca anyway, and in my total fascination with Takinaktu I found it easy to ignore him most of the time.

One night Takinaktu asked me, ''Why are you traveling with that man?''

''It's a long story. I met him in Mexico and fate has kept us together ever since.''

"I don't like him."

"Neither do I. And I doubt that he likes us much. But we can't get to Peru without him."

"Do we want to get to Peru?" she asked.

"Isn't that the whole idea? To have a palace in Cuzco—to share the treasures of the Incas—"

"You're being silly, Dan. You won't get any treasure. They'll probably arrest you before anything happens."

"I'm prepared to take the chance."

"I'd rather go somewhere else, though. England, maybe."

"England's a fine place," I said, "But I've been there and gone. I'm not going back until I'm a rich man."

"Is money that important?"

"Money. Power. Adventure. What else is there, really? When the time comes for the summing up, it matters only where you've been, what you've done."

Takinaktu shook her head. "What matters is the kind of person you have been. The pledges you've kept, the loyalty shown."

"You're a fine one to talk! Sneaking away from your family in the middle of the night! At least I told my people where I was going, and why."

"I had to leave. I could have never had my father's permission to go. Sometimes loyalty to self comes above other loyalties, Dan."

"Exactly. And out of loyalty to self I'm on my way to Peru to win—"

"To steal, you mean. To steal other men's treasure. But it won't work. Dan, forget Peru. Let's leave Manco and go someplace else."

"Where?"

"Africa, maybe. I've heard so much about Africa from the Russians. They say it's the coming place, the next dominant continent. Mexico, Peru, they're on the downtrend now. I'd like to be in Africa when the time of greatness comes."

Her enthusiasm was contagious, Instantly, Africa looked as appealing to me as Mexico had looked a year ago—a land of boundless opportunity and overflowing riches. But I had promised Manco Huascar to go with him to Peru. Little as I cared for him, I couldn't very well abandon him in the midst of nowhere and run off to Africa with Takinaktu.

And I couldn't get to Africa from the midst of nowhere, either. I would have to book passage from some port on Mexico's eastern coast, probably good old Chalchiuhcueyecan. So I began to assemble a plan. The three of us would continue south as far as Tenochtitlan. But in the Mexican capital would come a parting of the ways. Manco Huascar could continue westward toward Acapulco and his voyage to Peru. Takinaktu and I would go eastward toward Chalchiuhcueyecan and our voyage to Africa. I didn't know how we'd pay for our fare, but that was a problem to be faced at the proper moment.

Like most long-range plans, this one came to nothing.

It was May, and we were far to the south, nearing the borders of Mexico. The green table-land to the north had given way to a brown, sun-blasted desert. We were passing well to the east of the farming villages, or at least we thought we were. But without a compass it is not always easy to know where you are. Eager as we were to avoid encountering members of the Aztec garrison that patrolled this province, we ran right into them.

Or rather they ran right into us. Late one after-noon as we rode across a dusty plain in the full heat of the sun a party of horsemen appeared on the horizon. Nomad raiders, we thought, and got ready to defend ourselves.

They weren't nomads, though. They were Aztec soldiers in quilted cotton armor—eight of them.

"You're under arrest," they said, and we went peacefully.

TWELVE

EASTWARD HO!

THEY took us to Pecos, a large farming town centered around a handsome four-story mud building. It was, I later learned, the easternmost of these desert villages, eighty miles or so from the river along which the others are strung. In a cool ground-floor room the soldiers interrogated us.

I was afraid that they'd recognize Manco and me as members of the ill-fated band that had attacked the Taos garrison. But my fears were groundless; our invasion had come at night, and no one had seen our faces clearly. We were wanted for another reason. That is, Manco Huascar was wanted.

The Aztecs leafed through a bundle of official documents until they found one calling for Manco's arrest. The picture of him on it was a fair enough likeness. I got a look at the wording of the poster: approximately, Manco was wanted for espionage. He was in the pay of the Inca Capac Yupanqui, and had sent back to Cuzco all sorts of secret information.

"It's not so!" Manco protested. "I'm in exile from Peru! I wouldn't help them! I'm no spy!"

"Take him to Tenochtitlan for trial," the commanding officer said.

Manco was dragged away. "Arrest him too!" he screamed, waggling a hand at me. "He's another spy! He's a traitor to Mexico! He—"

The Peruvian vanished from sight.

All the pieces fit together, now. I saw why he had been so secretive about his personal background, and why he had been so curious about everything he saw. I understood, too, why we had made that long detour to Takinaktu's country. No doubt the Inca authorities had told him to sniff out the strength of the Russians up there. It struck me that Manco must have set up that whole visit of ours to the Russian stockade. All the time that I thought we were spying for Chief Tlasotiwalis, we were really spying for Peru!

But Manco was gone, now, and we were well rid of him.

The Aztec officer was staring curiously at Takinaktu and me.

"Well, now, what are we to do with you two? Who are you, where from, where bound?"

I showed him my tattered passport. "English traveler, sir. I've been in Tenochtitlan for a while. And now I'm heading for Africa."

"What about the girl?"

"She can't speak Nahuatl. She's from the village of Kuiu, on the coast of the Western Sea. Bound for Africa with me. She's got no papers, I'm sorry to say."

The Aztec gave us a nasty smirk. Well, let him draw any conclusions he pleased, I thought. He frowned for a moment and said, "Where are you planning to board ship?"

"Chalchiuhcueyecan, sir."

"The girl, too?"

"Yes, sir."

"But I can't let her into Mexico. She's got no papers."

"We're only in transit," I pointed out. "We're not going to settle there."

"How can I know that? The rules are the rules. It takes a passport to cross the border."

I hadn't thought of that. I stood there stymied. Takinaktu wanted to know what was going on, and I told her. She said, "Ask him if there's a port in the Upper Hesperides where we can get a ship to Africa."

I relayed the question. The officer thought a while, then produced a map of the hemisphere printed in smeary, garish colors. After puzzling over it a bit, he made a pencilmark on the eastern coast of the continent, just above that little south-eastern peninsula.

"Here," he said. "There is a port. Ships leave every month or so for Chalchiuhcueyecan. You can book passage there, shuttle down to Mexico, and board a ship for Africa there. Even without a passport you'll be able to stay at Chalchiuhcueyecan waiting for the first ship out. Of course, I don't know what will happen to the girl when she lands at Africa. They're likely not to let her in without papers. But perhaps you'll find a way around that by then." He grinned. "Good luck, anyway."

We had a hearty meal at Aztec expense, and got our horses scrubbed down in the bargain. The commanding officer, who was a good man but a stickler for the rules, did everything possible to make us happy—except let us into Mexico. He gave us maps, a compass, some provisions, even a little ammunition. I doubt that he'd have been so hospitable if he had known that I had been among the attackers at Taos.

Before we set out, Takinaktu and I studied our map carefully. We had nearly fifteen hundred miles to go, through territory that was under Aztec rule but inhabited mainly by woodland savages, except in the hundred-mile-wide strip paralleling the eastern coast where fairly sophisticated village-dwellers live. With luck, we could make the trip in five or six weeks, unless we ran into problems in the desert stretch just ahead. The desert tribes were said to be cannibals or head-hunters, maybe both.

Of course, there was nothing stopping us from riding east for a couple of days, then turning south and going down into Mexico. I would have loved to show Tenochtitlan to Takinaktu, and to have seen old Quequex again. But if someone in authority asked Takinaktu for her papers, we'd be in trouble. They would deport her—sending her out of the country the way she had entered it. We'd never get to the ports that way. It seemed simpler to head eastward.

There was another thing in mind. The port we were heading toward lay in the country of the Muskogee people. My shipboard friend Opothle was a Muskogee. If we took this route, I'd have a chance to see Opothle again and thank him for the knife that had been so useful to me.

That decided it. Eastward it was.

We rode out of Pecos the following morning and clattered through many miles of desert country before we halted and camped for the night. A spooky night we had of it, too. There was no moon, only the bright sparkling stars in a very black sky. The temperature fell sharply, as it often does on the desert even in summer. And from the distance came the weird and unsettling yipping of the prairie wolves, which the Mexicans call the coyotl. I cannot describe the howling of the coyotl, except to say that you do not fall asleep easily after you have heard those wild sounds moving along the rim of the world. I did my best to look brave and unconcerned. But I knew of the deadly wolf-packs that roam the thick forests of Europe, and I did not want to meet the coyotl at close range.

We took turns sitting watch that night. But the coyotl stayed away, and at dawn we breakfasted and rode on.

I felt ill at ease, now that I was alone with Takinaktu. She rode and used her bow and hacked up meat so efficiently that I forgot she was female from time to time. But not for long. Tough and durable though she was, she was still a girl, the most beautiful girl I had ever known, and I loved her for her toughness and for the way she read Shakespeare and for the way she looked, among a million other things, but I could never find the words to tell her any of it. I think she knew, though.

In any case, the absence of our chaperone Manco Huascar made things harder for us, not easier. We were both a little afraid of each other, I think, and also afraid of what it meant to be in love. So walls of wary self-consciousness sprang up between us. When we came to streams deep enough and clean enough to bathe in, Takinaktu went a mile up-stream from me, though it was dangerous to sepa-rate like that. At night we slept on opposite sides of the fire, even when it would have been better to huddle together against the cold. And when we talked, we let a kind of impersonal coolness creep in. It was easy enough to talk about Shakespeare, impossible to talk about how we felt about each other.

Why is it that two people who have every reason to drop all such barriers prefer to build them higher instead? I wish I knew. I wish I had that eastward journey to live over, too. I'd undo all my mistakes—the little ones of tactlessness and shyness, as well as the catastrophically stupid one that caused us to part.

Still, don't misunderstand: we enjoyed traveling together and we had a good time. I didn't miss Manco Huascar a bit. We spoke English as much as we could, Takinaktu improving visibly from day to day, and we whiled away the evening by translating *Romeo and Juliet* out of the original Turkish.

On the sixth day out from Pecos, the cannibals caught us.

The sky was blue and cloudless, the sun warm but not uncomfortable, and the brown plains seemed endless. Here and there a flat-topped hill sprouted from the earth. I was in a good mood, relaxed and cheerful, and we cantered along at a rapid clip.

"Look there," Takinaktu said suddenly.

I followed her pointing arm to the south, and saw a band of horsemen outlined against the deep blue of the sky. There must have been a dozen of them, and they were moving fast. I gave my horse some heel. Takinaktu did the same. But I didn't fool myself into thinking we would escape them.

"An Aztec patrol," I said encouragingly.

"Cannibals," said Takinaktu. She was never one for self-deception.

They were some miles away when we first saw them, for in that flat country the eye's reach is great. It took little time for them to get to us, though. In minutes they were wheeling around and around us, waving spears and hatchets and shouting hoarsely to us in some almost-Nahuatl dialect to halt.

Fierce is the only word for them. Naked but for a strip of skin around their waists, painted with bright stripes, thin-faced and wild-eyed, they looked every bit as barbaric as rumor made them out to be. For the first time since I had known her, I saw the shadow of fear on Takinaktu's face. Nor did I blame her much for fretting. Her life had begun anew when she had escaped from that squalid shoreside village, and she had not crossed an entire continent to finish so quickly as cannibal stew.

"What are they saying?" she asked.

"They want us to come before their chief. He'll judge us."

"And then what?"

"I don't know."

"Dan, will they eat us?"

"They might," I said. "I hear people taste good, with lots of salt and pepper in the pot."

It was a feeble attempt at humor, and it didn't amuse her much. Nor me. Our arms were trussed behind our backs, and cannibal braves flanked our horses, holding the reins and leading us to the camp somewhere in the south.

I had little hope that we would live through the night. As we jogged along I conceived various harebrained schemes, such as making a suicidal attempt to escape that would allow Takinaktu to slip away while I was being subdued. I doubted that it would work, but for at least a minute I was willing to try it. It would mean certain death for me, of course, and the thought that I might die in the next five minutes was as startling to contemplate as it had been the first time I realized that I might one day be a married man. But then I considered what was likely to happen to Takinaktu, wandering alone in this desert, and I decided to shun the heroics and hope for the best.

After riding for a cheerless hour we came to the redskin camp: a dreary array of flimsy deerskin tents, outside which some half-naked women and some all-naked children were doing household chores. I noticed without much pleasure a huge fire-pit filled with charred wood and what looked suspiciously like charred bones. A couple of boys were industriously erecting a thick pole in the middle of the pit.

The stake, I thought. For cooking dinner.

Takinaktu saw it too, and I looked at her face and then quickly looked away again, for I knew she did not want me to see her cry. She was not exactly crying, doing a good job of holding it in, with trembling lips and blurry eyes. I was proud of

her. I didn't know any other girl who wouldn't go
into hysterics at the sight of the stake she was
going to be burned at. For that matter, if Takinaktu
hadn't been with me I might have been going into
some hysterics myself. Obviously I didn't get
roasted, or I'd not be here to tell the tale, but I had
no way of knowing then that I would be spared.

The braves who had captured us began to dis-
cuss dinner plans with the women. They spoke in
a crude dialect of Nahuatl, but I got the drift of the
debate. Some of them wanted to cook me for
dinner and save Takinaktu to be a slave. Others,
objecting that I was all stringy muscle, wanted to
cook Takinaktu and make *me* a slave. Still others,
who must have had really good appetites, wanted
to cook both of us for tonight's meal.

In the end they worked out a cozy compromise.
Takinaktu would be cooked first, and I'd be held
in reserve. If the tribe was still hungry later, I'd go
on the fire too. Otherwise I'd be saved for the next
feast.

If there's anything I like less than the thought of
being burned alive, it was the thought of being
forced to sit by while watching Takinaktu cooking
at the stake. Gruesome and ghastly images went
through my mind; and as I saw her tender flesh
sizzling and blackening, I tried desperately to think
of something else, but the harder I attempted to
change the subject, the more grisly my imaginings
grew.

I think that was the most terrible moment of my

life. I came close to losing my mind altogether while those redskins calmly discussed the order in which we would be eaten. Their matter-of-fact tone lent a special touch of horror to it all.

But before either of us could go to the stake, the Chief had to approve. And the Chief, it seemed, was off on a hunting trip somewhere and might not be back till sundown, which was at least an hour away. Some of our friends did not want to wait that long; it takes time to cook a full-grown human being, and they were in a hurry to get the barbecue going. At one point it appeared as if they wouldn't wait. They laid hands on Takinaktu and began to haul her to the stake, while the women started stripping away her clothing. (I don't know whether it was because roasting deerskin smells bad or whether they wanted to use our clothes themselves, but they were going to strip us before they tied us up.)

Then—while some of them objected to the unseemly haste and others went right on preparing the firewood—a voice cried out, "The Chief is coming! The Chief is coming!"

Five horsemen galloped into the camp. Four of them were fiercely painted braves. The fifth was the Chief. He vaulted from his horse and walked toward us.

He was no desert redskin. He was tall and lean, with an Aztec's fluid grace of motion and an Aztec's glossy shoulder-length black hair.

He looked very much like an Aztec. He *was* an Aztec.

He was Topiltzin, as it happened.

"Dan!" he whooped. "How did you get here?"

I was too shocked to whoop anything. I just gawped foolishly at him.

"Untie them!" Topiltzin barked. "Hurry up, you fools! Free them both!"

"What's happening?" Takinaktu asked, as though in a dream.

"We're saved. The Chief's an Aztec friend of mine—or his ghost. That's Topiltzin, the one who led the attack on Taos."

"You said he was dead!"

"He doesn't seem to be. And it looks like we won't be, either."

Our bonds were loose. Takinaktu fixed her disarranged jacket. Topiltzin was belaboring the redskins in their own dialect, kicking them and shouting at them and otherwise expressing his outrage for what had nearly been done to us. And the cannibals took the abuse meekly.

"There is so much for us to say to each other," Topiltzin told me, "that I hardly know where to begin. I have a thousand questions to ask."

"And I have a thousand and one, Topiltzin."

"Come with me."

He led us both into his tent, which seemed no more impressive than any of the others. Our narrow escape had left me wobbly-legged, and I half stumbled to the floor. Topiltzin sat facing me, Takinaktu beside me. A woman brought us refreshments: a bowl of some sweet smelling green liquid, and chunks of dried meat. Takinaktu looked skeptically at the meat.

Topiltzin roared with laughter. "No, it's not human flesh!"

I repeated his assurance to her, and told Topiltzin, "She doesn't understand Nahuatl."

"Who is she? Your wife?"

"Not exactly. Not yet, anyway." I reddened and was glad Takinaktu couldn't understand me. "She comes from a village on the northwestern coast. That's where Manco Huascar and I feld after the attack—Kuiu, the village of Klagatch the medicine man. And when we left there, she wanted to come with us. So—" I hesitated. "But you can hear our story later. I want to know how you returned from the dead, and how is it we find you the chief of a cannibal tribe."

Topiltzin bit off a good piece of meat before he began to speak. He told his story swiftly, and I translated the important parts for Takinaktu.

Although badly wounded, he said, he had avoided capture by the Taos garrison by crawling into a ground-floor room of one of the village houses. The Taos people, hating the garrison as they did, had nursed him back to health, hiding him from the Aztec soldiers. Within a month the chest wound had healed and he was fit to travel.

He slipped out of Taos and went down to Picuris, where we had left our motorcars. The cars were still there. He picked the sturdiest, loaded its boiler with coal, and drove off to the east, planning to loop around Pecos and take the desert route back to Mexico.

But he had discovered Aztec patrols roaming the desert near Pecos—probably the same that had picked us up. So Topiltzin had simply continued driving east, intending to make a much bigger loop. About a hundred miles farther on he encountered the nomad people-eaters. Though he was armed, he fully expected to be captured and cooked as soon as his car ran out of coal, which would be fairly soon.

However, the chugging, smoke-belching motor-car awed the savages into a state of total aghastness. They had never seen such a thing before. They thought it was a demon, and Topiltzin, as a man who had tamed a demon and rode on its back, must therefore be something special. They fell on their faces before him and begged him to be their chief.

"So you got your kingdom after all," I said.

"Such that it is. Fifty savages, a dozen tents, and a heap of charred bones."

"Do you eat human flesh with them?"

"The taste grows on you," he said calmly.

"You've become a *cannibal?*"

"My people expect me to share their feasts. And there is little other food here. One becomes accustomed."

"How could you do it?"

"I tell you: one becomes accustomed. And you, Dan? What took you to the far north?"

I briefly outlined my recent travels, speaking of our three-man trek across the winter wilderness, Sagaman Musa's solo escape to the west, our adventures in and about Kuiu, our return, and Manco Huascar's arrest.

"And now?" Topiltzin said. "Bound for Africa, both of you?"

"To Africa, yes. Through the Muskogee country and by ship to Chalchiuhcueyecan, then across the Ocean Sea. We can't go via Mexico. Takinaktu lacks a passport."

"The Muskogee country, is it? I've often thought of going there, myself. Could you use an escort?"

"Meaning yourself?"

"Myself and my tribe. We'll see you safely to the eastern coast. With half a hundred cannibals to protect you, there'll be no dangers."

I wasn't too sure I wanted such fierce company on the trip. Yet many dangers lay before us. The resurrected Topiltzin offered protection, and after some thought I accepted.

"One more thing," he said. He reached around behind and opened a wooden chest that lay on the floor of the tent. "At Picuris I was able to obtain some of our expedition's baggage. This, for example."

He tossed me the battered little bag in which I had kept the things I had brought from England. He tossed me the ponderous jade necklace, Quequex' gift. He tossed me the sumptuous cape of feathers I had won in that bloody tlachtli game in

Tenochtitlan. I was as happy as I had been when we were rescued from the fire. I had never expected to see these things again.

Takinaktu's eyes were aglow with pleasure at the sight of the Aztec treasures. "Stand up," I said, and she did, and I draped the jade necklace over her shoulders. She fingered the polished green stone in awe. I put the gaudy mantle of feathers on her too, and she gasped in delight at its beauty.

"Such wonderful things! Where are they from?"

"Tenochtitlan. They were given to me there. My friend Topiltzin has kept them for me."

Topiltzin, as a matter of fact, looked rather displeased at what I had done. Among the Aztecs, the women stay to the background, and the men wear the long hair, the colorful robes, the intricate jewelry. Topiltzin could not understand why I had chosen to bestow my finery on this slender, pale female creature. I had no regrets, though. When I was in Tenochtitlan, I dressed as a man would dress in Mexico, and so I gloried in my newly-gained plumage. But it is not the normal custom of an Englishman to beautify himself in that way. Such treasures rightly belong to women. So, having no need to don the splendor of a Mexican male when outside Mexico, I turned cape and necklace over to Takinaktu and drew my pleasure from her wearing of them. She looked superb, too. Her simple buckskin costume was far from glamorous, but in these bright ornaments she took on an added warm glow of beauty that thrilled and delighted me. She wore them with pride. Perhaps she could ride a horse or shoot an arrow like a man, but when it came to an essentially female thing like this she turned out to be essentially female.

Topiltzin and I talked far into the night. Takinaktu, not understanding our words, sat by patiently, soothed by her gifts. At last we rose and went to the tents that were set aside for us. On our way, we passed the pit of charred wood and charred bones, and I shuddered a bit and walked quickly on.

THIRTEEN

SOMETIMES WE NEVER LEARN

THE journey to the eastern shores was a slow one, lasting many months, and I had ample time to think about where I had been and where I was going. We made good time on horseback, but since we moved with a family group it was necessary to halt each afternoon to pitch camp. I asked Topiltzin what had happened to the sacred motorcar; he said it had run out of coal long ago, and had been left to rust in the desert as an idol for nomads.

It was ten months since I had left England. In one sense I had done a great deal in that time, and in another sense I had done nothing at all. I was as penniless as when I started out. I had won no empires, not even a small and dusty province. I had covered a lot of territory, true, and seen some fighting, and killed some men and gained a scar. I had suffered, I had grown more shrewd, I had certainly gained in physical strength. As I summed it all, though, I saw that it added up to little. In terms of the lofty ambitions with which I had left home, it added up to zero. I had learned that the world is full of crafty folk and that energy and ambition alone are not enough to win an empire. I must readjust my sights downward somewhat. That in itself was knowledge worth the having, I suppose.

The balance sheet, then, showed only intangible assets gained on this venture: new toughness, new endurance, a greater knowledge both of my limitations and of my abilities, of my weaknesses and of my strengths. Perhaps Takinaktu might be listed as a more tangible asset, but in no sense could I truly say she was mine. We traveled together, we read Shakespeare and studied English together, and perhaps we loved each other; yet I knew she might drop from my world as abruptly as had Quequex or Manco Huascar or that girl at the inn on Chalchiuhcueyecan, never to be seen again. No formal bonds linked us.

Self-knowledge is a valuable thing, as is enhanced strength. Yet neither of them makes a particularly palatable meal. I was still a pauper. Now I proposed to leave the Hesperides and try my luck in Africa. What reason did I have to think things might be better there?

None.

What plans had I made for my future there?

None.

What ideas did I have for winning fame and wealth there?

None.

You see how it was. I had learned, and yet I had not learned, for I was preparing to come to Africa as blind as I had been when I landed in Mexico.

With these gloomy thoughts I diverted myself as our party jogged eastward along the lower haunch of the Upper Hesperides.

We were out of that desert now. We were in warm, wet country, almost tropically dank. The Gulf of Mexico lay to our right; to our left sprawled the eastern half of the continent, nearly an unbroken stand of virgin forest. Looking north into the pinedark hills, I hungered to make some use of that vast tract of land. The woodland folk live there: perhaps two million of them, spread over land that could support a population fifty times as great. They owe allegiance loosely to the Aztecs, and pay tribute. In the southeast, the natives are more strongly bound, and try to be imitation Aztecs themselves, building temple mounds of earth to copy the marble pyramids of Mexico. But in the unknown northeast the people of the forests are virtually independent. On the coast are a few trading posts run by Frenchmen and Spaniards, but they have nothing like the authority of the Russian trading posts on the other side of the continent. Thousands of square miles lay waiting to be tapped. A hundred Englands could be dropped down in that huge land. For a moment I thought, conqueror-fashion, of the use that Europeans could put this continent to, but then I remembered who I was and what I believed, and scoured the thought from my brain. Let the conquest of the Hesperides take place on the far side of the Gate of Worlds.

We did not eat human flesh as we traveled. At least, I hope not. I told Topiltzin that Takinaktu and I had moral, hygienic, and digestive objections to dining on longpork. He promised that we would get other meats. I do not know how well that promise was kept, but at least no human beings were roasted in my presence. It was the custom of this tribe to dine on hapless strangers several times a month, eating animals of the lower species the rest of the time. Sometimes at dinner we had steaks of an unknown kind, and I felt a bit queasy about them, but hunger prevailed over scruples. If through ignorance and Topiltzin's deceit I committed the sin of cannibalism, I hope the Lord will forgive me at the day of reckoning.

Late in June we came to the mighty, muddy Mississippi. The "Father of Waters," so this brown stream is known to the natives, and I believe it. They say there is a mightier river in Africa, and someday before long I hope to lay eyes on it, God willing; the Congo, it is. Tales are told of a river in the Lower Hesperides that dwarfs Congo and Mississippi together, and perhaps it does, though I'll never know at first hand.

For a price in meat, redskins ferried us across

the river. They were of the Choctaw tribe, akin to
Opothle's Muskogee folk. Civilized and courtly
they were, and in speech and dress they reminded
me of my three cabinmates on the ocean crossing.
The Choctaws looked upon Topiltzin's cannibals
with distaste, as well they might, for nothing is so
repellent as a member of your own race who lives
in barbarism. Topiltzin, though, they deferred to
with reverence, sensing that he must be an Aztec
of the royalty family. They regarded Takinaktu as
Topiltzin's princess, which aroused some jealousy
in me and some good-natured teasing from the two
of them. As for me, the Choctaws stared with
unabashed curiosity; Englishmen were rarities here,
and blond men as strange as five-legged storks.

When we were on the far side of the big river,
Topiltzin at last let me know why he had come
east with me.

I had been wondering about that. After all, we
hadn't been such great friends that there was any
motive for him to uproot his tribe from its tradi-
tional hunting grounds and parade more than a
thousand miles through unknown country. Protecting me couldn't have been that important to him,
nor was he here as a tourist.

He said, "These Choctaws are fine people, are
they not?"

I allowed that they were.

"To the north, here, we have the Chickasaws.
To the northeast, the Cherokees. To the east, the
Muskogees. All of them settled and civilized, all

of them related by custom and language. It's an attractive province, I'd say. How would you like to help rule it, Dan?''

"Rule it?''

"Rule it. It's the same story here as at Taos. There's only a token garrison occupying the entire province for Mexico. That's a mark of a dying empire, you know, when skelton platoons are left in charge of outlying territories. It means the empire's pulling in to its core. Rome did that, left the frontiers untended, and the barbarians—''

"Skip the history lesson, Topiltzin. What do you have in mind?''

"Conquer the garrison. Take over the land. Make ourselves monarchs here. We can do it easily.''

I scowled at him. "Sometimes we never learn, eh, Topiltzin? You propose to do exactly what you did at Taos. And it'll end the same way. Maybe the garrison is small, but it's made up of Aztec soldiers, and you've got nothing to throw against them but naked savages. Sorry. Count me out.''

"But sometimes we *do* learn, Dan! What was the real lesson at Taos?''

"That we should forget about trying to grab provinces of the Aztec empire.''

"No!'' Topiltzin's eyes glittered with strange fervor. "What I learned at Taos is that I should have taken Sagaman Musa's advice. I should have invited the subject populace to join the uprising. Instead I was too proud, too heroic to accept the help of mere farmers. I won't make that mistake again. These Choctaws and Muskogees will fight by our side, thousands of them. All they need is a leader, and they'll rise up and drive their overlords out!''

"It won't work, Topiltzin."

"Why not?"

"Because they won't risk their lives in a revolution only to replace one set of masters with another. If they toss out the garrison, do you think they'll elect you king?''

"I do. They aren't capable of ruling themselves, and they know it. They've been Aztec subjects for three hundred years. They need someone to make the decisions for them. I'll be available for that. So will you. Bit by bit, we'll become indispensable to them. Until I'm the king and you're my prime minister. We won't *force* ourselves on them. We'll slide gently into positions of permanent authority. As the heroes of the revolution, we'll be great men to them.''

"You be a great man without me," I told him. "I'm going to Africa with Takinaktu."

"Don't be a fool. This is the opportunity of your lifetime—it's what you've been looking for since you left England. Don't compound old errors by letting them guide you.''

"I saw one uprising fall flat on its face in Taos, Topiltzin. I got out of Kuiu before another one turned into a certain massacre. I don't want any part of this one.''

"But it's different here! Thousands of well-armed men on our side! We can't lose!"

"Do it without me. I'll read about it in the papers when I get to Ghana."

Topiltzin seized my arm as I walked away, and poured more persuasion into my ear. But I wasn't having any. I had nearly lost my life in Topiltzin's last wild scheme, and that was sufficient.

I felt very smug at having made a sensible choice for the first time in my life. I wanted someone to praise me for my shrewdness in turning Topiltzin down, so I went to Takinaktu and told her the story.

She pulled a long face during the first half of the tale, undoubtedly because she suspected I was working up to telling her that I was going along with Topiltzin. Then I sprang my surprise, quoting my pious rejection of his temptations.

Her eyes fluttered a bit. "You aren't going to do it?"

"No."

"Really?"

"Really."

"Oh, Dan, how wonderful! I was sure you would, and then you'd be killed, and everything would be ruined!"

She flung her arms around me. For one dizzying moment her lips touched mine and her soft, yielding body was deliciously close. Kissing is not a custom of her people, I understand; she must have learned such things from reading Shakespeare. In any case, it was a splendid thing, an unforgettable instant. I go back to it in my mind from time to time, since it is the high point of my friendship with Takinaktu.

After a high point usually comes a descent down the other slope. That's what happened. Let me tell it without skipping any of it, but also without drawing out the details too painfully.

Takinaktu let go of me and stepped back. That was the beginning of the downward slide. She looked shy and bewildered at what she had done. We grinned at each other a bit, and then she turned and loped off like a frightened doe. I rubbed my lips with my hand. They were tingling.

I told myself I had been wondrous clever to say no to Topiltzin. It was a sign of maturity. To abandon my folly of wealth through conquest meant I had grown up.

But if I was as mature as all that, why did I change my mind and go with Topiltzin after all?

The process of changing your mind is a tricky one. You start at Position A, which you hold with stern stubbornness, resolving never to give it up. Then you stop to question your original resolution. Is it wise to be so stubborn? Perhaps you should consider alternate ideas. You revise your original inflexibility a little, abandoning Position A and adopting Position B, which is very much like it in most ways, with only a few ifs and maybes added. Then, by a gradual series of compromises, private deals, and shifts of purpose, you slide spinelessly through the alphabet until you arrive at Position Z, the total opposite of your original point of view.

Something like that happened to me. I'll spare most of the intermediate stages, merely saying that I reconsidered. I began to think Topiltzin might just succeed. I remembered Opothle and his two companions, how strong and resilient they were, and how much they hated Aztec rule. I recalled my own dreams of empire and allowed that this particular part of the world was more desirable than most. I even felt that I had a certain obligation to go along with Topiltzin's plans, though I can't imagine why.

Inch by inch, I slid from A to G to M to P. And at Position P, I remained a while, more than half determined to join Topiltzin, but not yet letting anyone know about it.

The problem was Takinaktu. I knew she was opposed to any such enterprise, and that it would provoke a mighty quarrel if I asked her to approve of it. So over the next couple of weeks, as we moved eastward into Muskogee country and as I moved closer to Topiltzin's outlook, I delicately sounded Takinaktu out, trying to discern changes in her position.

Would she like to settle here instead of going all the way on to Africa?

Not very much.

How would she care to take part in a small battle or two?

Not really.

Wouldn't she like to win wealth and power? Elsewhere.

Of course, I tried to be more subtle than that. I didn't come right out and tell her what I had in mind. But she wasn't subtle at all in her answers.

And one day she said, "Dan, are you going to get mixed up in this war of Topiltzin's after all?"

I was flustered. I fished for words and caught none.

She went on, "I just want you to know, in case you're considering it, that I won't have any part of it. I'm going on to Africa, with or without you. Clear?"

I calmed her down with some vague assurances.

In my own smug way, I assumed she was bluffing. Since I loved her, I figured she therefore must love me just as much, and would never go through on her threat to sail to Africa alone. I was confident of bringing her around to our side—that is, if I decided I was on Topiltzin's side.

That decision was made when we were deep in Muskogee territory, less than two days' journey from the sea. We had passed any number of neat villages, each with straight, well-laid-out streets, a central plaza which had a temple mound at one end and a chief's house at the other, and carefully tended fields of tall corn on the outskirts. Green fields, blue sky, yellow sun, brown earth—a warm and lush land it was, far more appealing than any part of Mexico. I liked the moderate climate; even here in summer it was much cooler than lowland

Mexico, and without the thin, chilly air of the highland part. I could easily have ended my quest in this land.

Topiltzin sent for me one afternoon when I came back from a fishing trip. I went to his tent and found him in conference with a broadshouldered man in Muskogee costume.

The Muskogee looked up. I recognized him.

"Opothle!"

"Dan Beauchamp!"

We slapped each other's backs, pumped each other's hands, did a little jig of reunion. I pulled out my knife—his knife, really—and said, "This has saved my life a million times!" I let fly, sending it thwicking into the tent-pole. Opothle unsheathed a new knife of his own and tossed it after mine; it landed half an inch away and twanged a bit, the butts touching.

We retrieved our knives and embraced again.

Opothle said, "I knew you would visit us one day, Dan!"

"Believe me, I didn't expect to be here. But I'm glad I am." I turned to Topiltzin. "This man and I shared a cabin for a thousand years, it seemed, when we crossed the Ocean Sea. There were two others, also. How are they, Opothle? Well?"

His face darkened. He told me that one of our shipmates, the youngest one, was dead. He had liquored himself up at a festival and had slapped an Aztec officer; the Aztec had shot him where he stood. The other man was currently away, on a trade mission to the Mohawks in the north.

Topiltzin said, "I have spoken with Opothle about an uprising. He is no lover of his people's masters. He is with us, and pledges five thousand men from thirty villages."

Right then and there all my lofty resolutions evaporated. What had seemed like a vain and foolish endeavor suddenly took on a new look. Topiltzin had won strong allies. With this determined army, how could he lose against a garrison of several hundred men at best?

More than that: I put aside my childish dreams of becoming a prince in this land, and saw the campaign in a new light. It was a war of liberation. I would be fighting beside my friend Opothle to dethrone the imperial overlords and make his people free. As a descendent of Englishmen who had writhed under the lash of the Turk for four hundred years, I did not need the advantages of freedom advertised to me.

We had undertaken a sacred trust. Opothle and Topiltzin and I would begin the job of rolling back the cruel Aztec regime that had dominated the Upper Hesperides so long. The glorious revolution would begin here, and would spread throughout the country in one thunderclap of rebellion. Solemnly we grasped hands on it. I knew now how the soldiers of James the Valiant had felt in their war against the Turk.

In short, I had arrived completely and irrevocably at Position Z.

Opothle had brought tobacco, and we smoked a few pipes to celebrate our alliance. Then he left, and I went to tell Takinaktu all about it.

I was puffed up with the nobility and grandeur of it all. And, despite her earlier hostility, I was certain she'd catch the martial spirit. She herself came from a nation that had lost its freedom; she would understand Opothle's yearnings and our eagerness to aid him.

I told her what had been decided and waited for her to fling her arms up and kiss me again.

Instead her face grew stony and she said, "This is a very poor joke."

"It's no joke at all."

"You really mean to stay here and fight?"

"That's right, Takinaktu."

There was fury in her eye, and I thought she had never looked so beautiful before. She said, "This is not your war. You'll get nothing from it but your grave."

"Opothle is my friend. But for his knife, I'd have found my grave two thousand miles west of here."

"There is no magic in his knife. Any knife would have been just as useful."

"That's not the point. His people are enslaved by the Aztecs. This is their time of freedom. How can I ignore that? How can I sail off, knowing that I've failed to help them throw of the Aztec yoke?"

"Topiltzin himself is an Aztec," she reminded me. "He dreams of being king. You would replace one master with another."

"No. He's a very unusual Aztec, Takinaktu. He doesn't care for his family. He's more or less an exile. He doesn't have any of the proper patriotic Mexican ideas. That's why he's willing to overthrow the garrison here. Afterwards, do you think he'll be able to push anyone around? He'll be part of the government, yes, but he won't be a dictator. And we'll be part of the government too."

"Perhaps you. Not I."

"But—"

"This is not my war, even if you think it's yours, Dan. I want to get far away from this continent where one race must own another. I want to go to Africa, where men are free, where each nation observes its own boundaries, where science and art are alive. This place means nothing to me."

"It means something to me, though. You were willing to run off and let your own village get shot up by the Russians. Well, that was a hopeless fight, but this one isn't. I'm staying, Takinaktu. I have to."

"Fool! Idiot!" she spat at me.

"Please. Stay here with me."

She drew herself up to her full height, looking proud and imperious in the jade necklace and feather cape I had given her. There were razor-keen edges on her words as she said, "Tomorrow I ride to the port and buy passage on the next ship to Mexico. At the Mexican port I buy passage to Africa. It was good to know you, Dan. Maybe some day we will meet again, if you survive this foolish war.''

She strode away.

I shook my head. Women! But despite her threat, I felt sure that she'd back down and stay here for the battle. I was wrong.

In the morning, she was gone.

Sometimes we never learn.

FOURTEEN

To Africa, I Think

WHEN she failed to appear for breakfast, I went to her tent. No Takinaktu. Necklace, cape, Shakespeare, and all, she had disappeared. I ransacked the blankets, looking for some note from her. Nothing. She had kept her word.

I wanted to claw down the sky in my anguish. Stupidly, I had let myself get entangled in a war and thereby lost the only person on this continent who really meant anything to me. In that first moment of shock I thought of saddling my horse and riding after her to the port, before it was too late, before she sailed away out of my life forever. But that would have been a betrayal of Opothle and Topiltzin. I had promised them my help. Could I run off after a girl at such a time?

243

I think I might have gone, torn as I was between my loyalty to this war and my need for Takinaktu. But a sturdy figure came up behind me and seized my wrist in a gentle but firm grip. Opothle. He knew nothing of the missing girl; his mind was all filled with war.

"Are you ready, Dan?" he asked quietly.

"Is today the day?"

"Today. No point in delaying. I have spent all this night gathering my men. Today we strike."

How could I tell them that I was sick to the heart over a runaway girl? Perhaps Takinaktu was still bluffing. Perhaps she was waiting a few miles to the east, hoping that I would ride after her. But I knew that if I rode out and looked for her and found her, I would ride with her straight to the port, forgetting all about Opothle's people and their war.

I could not do that. It would be too harsh a betrayal.

Topiltzin, that sly devil, had thoroughly entangled me in the morality of this campaign. It was not like the attack on Taos, a mere power grab. No, this had become a sacred war. My heart was riding eastward to the sea, but I had to remain and fight.

I remained. I fought.

When I saw the Muskogee army, I felt certain we would win. I should have mistrusted any feeling of certainty at all, after my reversals of recent days, but these men looked invincible. Thousands of them, strong, young, a copper-skinned army,

bristling with knives and war-hatchets and rifles
and small arms, their faces set in grim determination.
Topiltzin and Opothle rode at the head of the
force, and I, a general at not-quite-nineteen, was
summoned up there to join them.

We discussed strategy. The plan was simple
enough, and had a certain familiarity about it. We
were to ride to the garrison, throw flaming torches
through its windows, and smoke the enemy out.
That scheme had not worked well at Taos. But
here we outnumbered the Aztecs twenty to one.
How could we lose?

We rode on, through the green fields of corn, to
wipe out the oppressors.

The Aztec fort was a squat, rambling brick building set in the midst of a broad clearing of red
earth. A low, futile wooden palisade surrounded
it. We came swarming up on all sides, having sent
scouts forward to make sure we would fall into no
traps.

Our corps of sappers began undermining the
palisade. It gave, and suddenly there was a breach
wide enough for horsemen to ride through six
abreast. Rifles high, we entered and readied ourselves to meet the counterattack. Our corps of
torchmen took the lead, heading for the windows.

We expected Aztec troops to pour out of the fort
to meet our thrust. We were wrong.

From one of the windows poked the gray metal
snout of a big cannon. Hiding a cannon indoors is
an unfair way of battle, but there it was.

Boom!

A hole was carved in our ranks.

Boom!

Boom!

Boom!

As a veteran of two disastrously mismanaged attacks, let me tell you that it is less easy to rout an Aztec garrison than one might think. That cannon unloaded explosive shells in our midst with improbable rapidity, and each time a shell landed some fifty of our warriors went up in a cloud of black smoke.

Behind the heavy artillery came a peppering of rifleshot. Our men dropped steadily. Brave as they were, it was hard for them to stand to such slaughter. They began to melt away into the surrounding woods.

I heard Opothle shouting to them, rallying them. The palisade was on fire, now, and in a while the fort would be open to easy attack. All we had to do was fall back beyond the range of that stubby cannon and pump bullets into the building. By and by the defenders would run out of ammunition.

But the Muskogee braves, beaten down by three hundred years of oppression, could not see the clean logic of that proposition. Some were fleeing as fast as they could; others were milling about aimlessly, ignoring the attempts that Opothle, Topiltzin, and I made to rally them.

Then a bullet smashed into Topiltzin's skull and the war was over.

I can't say I had ever actually liked the amibitious Aztec very much, but I had followed him into battle twice—three times, if you count that game of tlachtli—and it pained me to see him die. Especially since this was the second time I had seen his death. From this one, though, there would be no ressurection. He lay in the dust with a bright scarlet thread of blood winding through his glossy black hair, and he did not move.

Topiltzin had been the prime mover of this attack, and when he fell the courage seemed to leave the others. Those that had remained to fight now fled. I saw Opothle, his face black with anger, pummeling his own tribesmen and urging them to stay at their posts, but it was no good. Within minutes, scarcely any of them were left, and there was nothing to do but flee ourselves.

Opothle rode off to the north. I had no chance to speak to him, and now I suppose I'll never see him again.

I fled the scene of the disaster in an easterly direction, of course. My goal was the coast, the port, the ship that would take me to Mexico and then to Africa.

I rode a weary horse, but I flogged it onward. The sun was high in the sky; it was late afternoon, and Takinaktu had had at least eight hours of head start on me. I still thought I could catch her in time. If not, perhaps no harm would be done, since from what I heard this was a sleepy little port from which ships sailed only every week or two.

She'd probably be at the harbor, waiting for the next sailing.

But after I'd ridden to twilight, I realized my horse might die underneath me if I pushed it further. I found a town, sold my horse, bought a new one with the money and some extra, and got on the road again. Darkness descended. I cursed myself six times over for a fool, letting Takinaktu slip away while I took part in that foredoomed battle.

And yet I knew I had done the right thing. If I had run off with a girl and ignored Opothle's bid for freedom, my conscience would have pained me to the end of my days. I had done the honorable thing, and it had failed, and now, if there was any justice in the universe, I would find Takinaktu waiting for me.

Night came, and with it heavy rains. I stopped in a village and got shelter till morning. It was useless to force myself on down the muddy road in darkness; horses stumble in the dark, and the risks outweighed the gains. Even if Takinaktu had reached the port town, her ship wouldn't depart in the night, and I'd have time to board it in the morning.

I rose at dawn. I spurred my horse mercilessly toward the shore. I got there while morning mists hung over the sleepy town, and rode out to the rotting piers, and asked someone official when the next ship left for Chalchiuhcueyecan.

"In three weeks," he said.

I let out a long sigh of relief. All my furious hurry had been needless! Three weeks, three weeks, three weeks! That meant Takinaktu must still be here, in some hotel, waiting for that distant sailing!

It was not hard to find the right hotel. There was only one in town.

I said to the woman in charge, "I'm looking for a girl with pale skin, sharp cheekbones, and dark hair. She may have been wearing a jade necklace and a feather cape."

"Yes, yes, she was."

"You've seen her? Where is she?"

"She was here yesterday. She arrived late in the afternoon."

"Yes, and now?"

"She sailed last evening for Mexico."

I turned away, unheroic hot tears stinging my eyes and a frenzied pounding within my chest. Sailed! Sailed last evening! Here and gone!

Now I knew why there would be no ship for Chalchiuhcueyecan for three more weeks. I had missed the last one by the space of a single day, and missed Takinaktu with it.

I had said that if there was justice in the universe, I would have found her waiting. Is there justice?

I booked a room for myself at the hotel. Then I walked back down to the wharf and found the same man I had spoken to before.

"You saw the boat leave for Mexico last night?"

"Yes."

"Was there a strange girl aboard it, a beautiful pale girl in Aztec jewelry?"

He smiled. "Yes, yes, there was. I saw her. A bride for a prince, that one!"

Some impulse unloosed my tongue and I blurted the entire story out to him. He listened sympathetically, for the harbor was quiet today and he had nothing else to do. At the end of it he tugged his chin and said, "She goes to Africa, you say? And you mean to follow her?"

"That's right."

"Perhaps you have a little luck left after all, then. In ten days there'll be a cargo vessel in this port, bound direct for Ghana. It won't stop first in Mexico. I'll get you aboard as a passenger, and you'll probably be in Africa only a few days after she gets there."

"Wonderful!"

"Of course, your passport had better be in order. The Africans are very strict about that. They won't let you in without proper papers."

I groped in my clothing to make sure I still had the weathered bit of paper, after all my wanderings. I did. Then I thought of something else.

"Takinaktu has no passport!"

"Then she'll never enter Africa."

"What will they do with her?"

"Keep her in detention at the port until there's another boat back to the Hesperides." He laughed. "Do you know what will happen? Your own ship will be the next boat, and so that will be the one on which they send her back! As you get off the ship, you'll see them bundling her aboard."

I didn't think that was funny at all. "There's no way she can get into Africa? She'll have to go back?"

"One way."

"Tell me!"

He leaned close to me. "If you marry her you can both travel on the same passport."

It is now the middle of July, 1986. In another few weeks I will celebrate my nineteenth birthday. If the Lord is with me, for a change, I'll celebrate it in Africa. And I'll celebrate it with Takinaktu— my bride.

I cannot be sure, of course. She may have talked her way past the customs shed and by now has disappeared deep within that continent. But I hope to find her waiting in detention, probably very angry with the world, expecting immediate deportation. And I will tell her the one way she can escape being shipped back to the Hesperides, and we shall see what happens then.

Right now I am on a ship, of sorts. A slow, creaking vessel toiling eastward with great strain. We have been at sea for two weeks now, and many weeks of voyaging lie ahead. I am the only passenger. The crewmen do not make good company, nor am I eager to talk to the cargo of pigs in the hold.

So I have been writing this memoir. Actually, I began it at the port, to while away the endless hours before my ship sailed. Now I continue it, scribbling twenty or thirty pages each day. It is a bulky manuscript. In it I have set down a little of myself, who I am and where I have been, in the hopes that I will understand myself a bit better. If I ever meet Takinaktu again, I will show it to her, so that perhaps she'll understand me better too. Besides, she has good literary judgment. If she thinks other people might be interested in this rambling account of my adventures, I may try to have it published. But all that is far off, now.

It is hardly satisfying to end a work like this with the hero still searching for the heroine, with no assurance that he will ever find her. But so it must finish. As of now I know nothing of the outcome. Though it is rash to feel sure of anything that lies in the future, I believe that I will find Takinaktu again, and that she will forgive me for staying to fight, and that I will forgive her for running off, and all will be well.

Meanwhile I use old Quequex' useful notion of a Gate of Worlds. With eyes closed I stand at that Gate, seeing past the golden radiance into other worlds of maybe. I see a world in which Takinaktu and I did not quarrel at the end, but sailed to Africa together. I see a world in which Topiltzin lived, and gained the kingdom he desired. I see a world in which each man is his own master, and there are neither conquerors nor conquered. I see many worlds beyond that Gate. And there is one in which Takinaktu and I lived happily ever after.

Perhaps. This old ship moves steadily eastward. To Africa. To Takinaktu. To a new life.

To Africa!